Class 2137

"When your time comes to die, be not like those whose hearts are filled with fear of death, so that when their time comes they weep and pray for a little more time to live their lives over again in a different way. Sing your death song, and die like a hero going home."
-Tecumseh

I

The 6am wakeup call over the intercom is more annoying than usual today, mostly because I was having such an amazing dream. I dreamt I was in the outside world, laying in the middle of a grassy plain on a nice summer day with the sun beating down on my skin. There was no one else around, no people, no animals, nothing, not even a sound aside from the gentle breeze coming across the plains. This was heaven in my mind, to be free of this place, to be able to completely relax without a care in the world and know that everything will be ok. Sadly, my perfect dream would have to be interrupted by yet another day of education and training, perhaps my sanctuary will allow me to return the next time my head touches my pillow. Until then however, I must face another day in the life, another day just like all the rest. That's when I hear my bunkmate Clarence, a 5'11" black 17 year old with brown eyes, and a shaved head, chime in, "Hey man, Happy Birthday Royce. One more to go."

Birthdays have never really been a means for celebration around here, especially when you are only guaranteed 18 of them. I read that the outside world actually enjoys birthdays, and loved ones bring presents and sing to you while throwing a party in your honor. This is a strange concept for me to try and grasp, but I guess it makes sense if you have 100 years to look forward to. Today marks the 17th year of my existence, which means that I have but one year left to prepare before I am put to the test. One more year before I am forced to enter the arena.

"Come on man," Clarence says, "let's go, I don't want to have to wait in line for breakfast." He's already dressed and ready to go. I find it annoying that some people are awake and ready before the wake-up call. I find it especially annoying that he looks as though he has even taken a shower before changing into his gym uniform- black shorts and a crimson athletic shirt. I just glare at him to try and convey as much as possible how thrilled I am to be awake and not sleeping.

"Give me a minute," I respond as I sit up, "it's my birthday and I'll take my sweet time if I want to."

"Seriously though," Clarence insists, "I'm starving, and if you don't get out of that bed I'm gonna have to drag you out. Don't think that blonde hair and those baby blue eyes are gonna stop me either, you aren't that cute. Get your skinny white butt in gear."

"It's too early for you to be so uppity," I groan as I jump down from the top bunk. I take a moment to throw my arms out to the side and stretch out before I walk over to my dresser and put on my gym uniform since it's our first class after breakfast. Life at the academy hardly leaves you with any free time, everything is scheduled from the time you show up clear through your 18th birthday. But hey, they give us 6 hours of free time every evening, so we've got that going for us, which is nice.

"Waiting on you, slowness," Clarence says while leaning on the wall next to the door to our room. I roll my eyes as I finish tying my shoes and stand up. Clarence has a big grin across his face, he thinks he's hilarious, but in the morning I consider him a real jerk.

As I walk towards the door and open it Clarence follows me out and throws his arm around my shoulders, "Cheer up man, you only turn 17 once, gotta enjoy the little things."

"I'm gonna enjoy kicking your butt in weights today, if that's what you mean," I say with a grin.

"That's more like it!" Clarence cheers, "But I don't know about that, today is chest and tri's, ain't no way you're benching more than me baby." He bounces his pecs at me as he says it with a huge smile across his face.

"Aren't you supposed to let me win since it's my birthday?" I ask.

"I don't think I could live with myself if I benched less than you," He replies.

"Yeah whatever," I say, "Someday you'll be big like me, someday Clarence."

The walk to breakfast isn't far at all, we're lucky enough to have a dorm room on the bottom floor right next to it, so we just have to walk a short distance down the white hallway outside of our room. As soon as we enter the cafeteria we get in line. There aren't too many people in front of us, breakfast is an hour long and it's only five minutes past the wake-up call. One by one we all step onto the scale and we're scanned. The scale is a three square feet metal plate in the ground that we step onto and face forward. In front of us is a black ball suspended from the ceiling with a red glass front, next to it is a computer screen. We have to stare into it so it can perform a retinal scan in order to identify who we are, it does a full body scan and measures exact height, body fat percentage, and lean body mass. It then looks up our schedule for the day to determine our projected activity level before the next meal, and then using the measurements it takes along with the weight taken from the scale it determines our exact macronutrient needs. Once we step off the platform a tray pops out in front of us with a bottle of water, a spoon wrapped in a napkin, and a pasty substance that contains the exact carbs, protein,

5

and fat that the computer determines that we need, as well as all the vitamins and minerals we need. The academy calls it a "super food", but after 17 years of eating the same thing three times a day, I am pretty sick of it.

The one thing I do look forward to this year, is that six months before you turn 18 they switch you to real food. All meals are prepared by an actual cooking staff, though still catered to your needs based off of your daily scans. Just six more months and I will get to try real food for the first time. From what I hear, real food is bursting with delicious flavors. Just six more months before I get to see for myself.

Clarence is first, as it scans and identifies him his information pops up on the screen.

> Clarence 2137
>
> Eyes: Brown   Hair: Black
>
> Height: 5'11"   Weight: 179 lbs
>
> Body Fat: 5.3%   Lean Body Mass: 169.5 lbs

After Clarence stepped off it was my turn.

> Royce 2137
>
> Eyes: Blue   Hair: Blonde
>
> Height: 6'1"   Weight: 187.5 lbs
>
> Body Fat: 6.67%   Lean Body Mass: 175 lbs

Everyone in the academy is extremely fit, it's normal for us since we have been in fitness classes since we could walk, but apparently it's abnormal for the outside world. I find that strange. Outside the academy everyone just seems so average and out of shape, at least they do on the TV. I read in my studies that apparently at one point over two-thirds of America was considered overweight, this was a long time ago but it's still a strange concept for me. I've never seen anyone in person that was out of shape, only on the TV.

Another big difference between us and the outside world is how everyone at the academy shares last names based on their birth year, whereas there are so many different last names outside. In the academy last name simply signifies your birth year, outside the academy you learn that last names are only shared with family.

"Fatty." Clarence jokes as I step off and grab my tray.

"Shortty," I retort with a half-smile. He scoffs as though he is offended, and we each let out a quick laugh.

We sit down at an empty table, our friends don't usually get to the cafeteria until breakfast is almost over. They have their fitness classes later in the day so they shower and such before breakfast.

We don't talk while we eat, not exactly much to talk about or comment on when you have had the exact same meal thousands of times before. By now all of the jokes about the food are just lame, and there is no point in really making them. We each just sit here and devour our paste in silence, plus the sooner we finish the more time it'll have to digest before we have to lift.

We're done by 6:30am, which leaves us 40 minutes to get to the weight room. There is a 10 minute grace period between meals and class, and it's only a 5 minute walk, so we aren't concerned with time. We each just get up and clear our trays and sit back down. "So how does it feel?" Clarence asks, "Just one more year before you gotta step up."

"Just another day in paradise," I say. I'm trying not to think about it, but Clarence seems insistent on bringing it up. I mean really, who wants to talk about what could possibly be their last year alive? Maybe it's because he was in this same position a little over two weeks ago. I am kind of down about it, but it doesn't really bother me too much. As long as I keep myself occupied, and keep moving forward, not thinking about it, I will be fine. Everyone has their own beliefs about death, some believe in a religious afterlife, others believe in ghosts. When it comes to me, I don't know that I believe anything, I just know that when you die that's it, that's the end of the road. And maybe that's all there is to it. Not knowing for sure if anything actually happens leads me to believe that nothing happens, and that scares me.

One of the first things that they try to teach you at the academy is to not fear death, that it can make you weak and cause you to freeze in the heat of combat. In my mind, it's the opposite. My fear of death is what drives me to work hard, harder than most. When it comes time to fight, and I'm out there in front of everyone with my life on the line, it's my fear of death that is going to push me to fight until my very last breath in order to survive. It's not the fear of not knowing what will happen when I die that drives me, sure that's part of it, but what really motivates me is not wanting to let my friends down, not wanting to lose them. I may not have much, but what I do have means everything to me.

I can feel my heart rate starting to rise, every time I let myself get too deep into thought about death I start to have a miniature panic attack. I'm pathetic. "Ladies," I hear a voice say as a tray slaps down on the table next to me. "Is this seat taken?" The voice belongs to Joseph, a 5'9" 16 year old white boy with short brown hair and green eyes. Right alongside him is his bunkmate Gordon, also 16 but with an olive complexion, short brown hair and brown eyes, standing at 6'0" tall. "How are we doing on this fine morning?"

"You've been spending too much time with Gordon," Clarence says. "His bad jokes are starting to rub off on you." Joseph grins and rubs the back of his head.

"Yes, how is everyone on National Freedom Day?" Gordon chimes in as he sits down. "I feel like there is something else significant about today too, but I can't put my finger on it... February 1st... OH YEAH! It's National Working Naked Day too!" Gordon always manages to take smart mouth to the next level,

8

he is also the king of random facts that no one cares about. While some of us train with our free time every evening, he spends his time in the Learn Smart zone looking up this type of stuff.

"Too bad neither of those stupid holidays apply to us," Clarence says.

"Well the naked one could," Joseph starts, "but you might catch some flak for that from the orderlies." He gestures toward the far corner at one of them. The orderlies are essentially the security/rule enforcers of the academy. With thousands of students running around they have to have some way of keeping us in line. The orderlies are all huge men dressed in off-white khakis, and tucked in royal blue polo shirts with black shoes. They look nice, but if there is ever a disturbance they get intimidating quick. Otherwise they are not permitted to interact with the students. Even if the orderlies don't see you doing something, there are also cameras throughout the compound, if they catch you doing anything out of line or unruly you will be disciplined. Their go to method of discipline is the box. The box is basically solitary confinement. You are put in a metal box barely big enough for you to fit in, with no light, no sound, nothing. Depending on the severity of your offense you can spend anywhere from an hour or up to six hours in the box. In really extreme cases they will stick you in there for multiple days in a row. They can't afford to have you miss training so they will allow you to go to your regular classes and meals and then you will be sent to the box until lights out. Most all of us take a trip to the box at some point when we are young, but usually one or two times is enough for you to never want to do it again.

"I'd rather keep my clothes on," Clarence states, "Royce doesn't need to see that stuff on his birthday.

"OHHHHHH, that's right it's his birthday," Gordon says, "I knew I was forgetting something. So how does it feel to be in your final leg of the race that leads to the arena?" Why is it that everyone is bringing up that I have a year left, I feel like if someone had just been stabbed you wouldn't immediately walk up to them and ask if

9

they were aware that they had a blade penetrating their body, as if they didn't already know.

"How about you tell me when you find out next month?" I tell Gordon, "Or you can ask Joseph the week after if you can't figure it out for yourself."

"OH!" Clarence yells.

"I've actually decided to put off turning 17 for a few more years," Gordon says, "but I'll let you know how it feels if I ever decide to age again." Everyone laughs.

"Let me know how that works out for you," I respond.

"Ditto," Clarence says.

We all like to joke about it, but everyone is scared on some level of entering the arena, it's almost all you can think about up until you turn 18. It's always in the back of your mind somewhere. At first you are confused and think 'why me?' Then you are just angry and act out, which the box quickly fixes, and then you just learn to accept that eventually it's going to happen and there is nothing you can do about it.

"Well if you two will excuse us," Gordon starts, "we have a most delicious meal prepared for us this morning, and would like to enjoy it in private. So if you could please vacate our table it would be appreciated." He flips his hand at us as though he is shooing us away.

"Yeah whatever," I say, "I'd rather spend my birthday in the gym than with you two clowns." Clarence and I get up and start to walk towards the exit.

"Happy birthday Royce," Joseph says with a smile as we're leaving, "I know it's rough, but try to enjoy it at least a little bit. Today is your day." Joseph has a smile that is impossible to not smile back at, a smile that even when you're furious about something it can immediately change your mood. Every time he smiles he does it with everything he has, you can tell it's real from ear to ear, and he always closes his eyes when he does it. His smile just fills you with warmth and helps you forget all the problems in life. Joseph is the most genuinely nice guy I know, if any of us are too good for this place, it's him.

"Thanks man, I'll do my best." I smile back at him, but as I turn away the smile fades. Even Joseph's ray of sunshine isn't quite enough to brighten this cloudy day.

We still have 15 minutes before the hour, so we're in no hurry to get there. We walk slow. "Hey man," Clarence says, "I know it sucks, I've been there. You gotta just buck up and take things as they come to you. Don't worry too much about it, the arena is future Royce's problem, let present Royce worry about stupid stuff like all the girls we aren't gettin', or hitting a new PR on bench press today." Clarence can always tell when something is on my mind, we have been bunkmates since we were five.

Your bunkmates are chosen the day you show up based on who showed up last or who shows up right after you. The only times you are matched with someone else is if there is a suicide, which was the case with both Joseph and Gordon, or in rare cases where some of the more rebellious kids who don't fall into the mold set by the academy are taken to the box and just don't come back. Each of Gordon and Joseph's roommates committed suicide within a week of each other, so they were put together when they were 11. It was a much more rare case for Clarence and me. Up until I was five years old I had a roommate named Lawrence, and he was one of the few who just refused to do what he was told. Lawrence was a kind soul and just refused to fight, he couldn't bring himself to hurt others no matter how bad they hurt him. I tried to tell him he needed to do what they said and be just like everyone else, but he just couldn't bring himself to do it. He was sent to the box on a daily basis, and then one day he just didn't come back. That night I didn't sleep, I just lay in bed waiting for him, but he never came.

The day after that Clarence was assigned to my room. Apparently Clarence's parents tried to hide him from the government and gave birth to him in secret, and then they tried to raise him within the confines of their home. This worked for a while, but eventually someone found out and when they faced fines or jail time the Academy stepped in and brought Clarence here. He doesn't like to talk about it too much, he didn't even really get to experience the outside world because he was never allowed to leave his home for fear that he would be discovered, but you can tell some of it has stuck with him. The way he talks and some of his mannerisms are just slightly different than most of us who have been here since birth.

I still remember when he walked in the room for the first time with an orderly. "This is your new roommate, Clarence. He will be in every class with you effective immediately."

"What about Lawrence?" I asked.

"Lawrence is none of your concern, just make sure to help Clarence out until he gets the hang of things." With that the orderly closed the door and it was just Clarence and I.

"Hi, I'm Clarence."

"I'm Royce, nice to meet you."

"Nice to meet you too, I think we're gonna be best friends."

"What makes you say that?"

"Well, I ain't never really had a friend before 'cept my momma and my family, so I figure that makes you my best friend." I was confused by him talking about his mom, how did he know his mom when no one else does? I was also thrown off by the declaration of friendship.

"Yeah okay, but my best friend is Lawrence so you're going to have to be better than him if you want to be my best friend, because I can only have one okay?"

"Maybe we can all be friends, maybe Lawrence will like me too. But if not that's okay, I won't be here too long. I'm just here for a little while until I can get out and see my momma again. They said I won't be able to see her for a while, and that I had to win a bunch of competitions to be able to see her, so I'm gonna have to work real hard so I can make it back to her!" He had a big smile on his face when he said this. I had lived my whole life up to this point in the academy, I knew exactly what we had to do in order to earn our freedom, even at five years old. Clarence didn't seem to understand yet though, either that or they just didn't explain it to him very clearly. He didn't know that he was stuck here for at least 13 more years, and then he would have to fight for his freedom. He didn't understand that we were essentially slaves with a grim outlook. He seemed so happy, and I was already seeing the world as a terrible place even at a young age. I wasn't sure at the time if he was stupid, or just optimistic, but I liked his energy. Even if he didn't know what he was getting into, he made it sound easy. It made me wonder if he might be right about us being best friends after all.

"We can talk later, hurry up and get changed so we can go eat breakfast." I didn't know it at the time, but Clarence was right, we did become best friends. I had never met someone who had such energy and drive. It took him a few days to get the hang of things and fall into the routine, and months to catch up to everyone else in their development, but he was never discouraged. He always kept his eye on the prize, getting out and finding his mom. He didn't have the same outlook about how he wouldn't be here long after finding out how things worked, but that didn't put a damper on his motivation. If anything I think it made him work harder, and I admired that. At first I kept waiting for Lawrence to come back, but eventually I accepted that it wasn't going to happen, but Clarence filled the void left by Lawrence and then some. It's hard not to be best friends with someone who is always the hardest worker in the room, someone who always exudes positive energy, and someone who is always there for you if you need him.

Clarence still talks from time to time about how he wants to find his mom when he gets out and tell her that he knows she did her best and it's not her fault. That's one thing that separates him from the rest of us, or at least me for sure. When I get out I won't go looking for my parents, most of us are in here because our parents didn't want us, or couldn't afford to keep us, or maybe they just plain got pregnant for a paycheck in the end. Regardless of the circumstances I can't forgive someone who chose to give their child a prolonged death sentence. Ultimately I'm glad that Clarence came into my life though, the academy believes that long term companionship through the years increases happiness as well as performance. I can honestly say that I would have a hard time if I didn't have Clarence, and I'm pretty sure the same goes for him.

"Yeah man," I say, "I just have to hit the weights hard, I always feel better after I lift."

When we get to the weight room we check in via retinal scan like every class and head over to the bench press. The academy starts you in weights as soon as you are coordinated enough to hold them, and they map out every single workout for you up until your 16th year. Once that happens they start to give you some freedom and let you choose what you want to do, so long as you are making progress. The staff monitors your daily scans to track progress and make sure you are adding to your lean body mass, if they see a decline they intervene and start programming for you again. Clarence and I decided on a P/P/L split once we had the freedom to do so, we train chest, triceps, and shoulders day one, then back and biceps day two, then finally legs and abs day three, and then we start again from the top. The academy doesn't allow days off, you are expected to lift seven days a week. The super food that we eat supposedly makes it so we can't over train, and thus far I've never experienced any problems.

The best part of the day is weights, every day no matter what. Part of it is because it is good stress relief, but the main part is the girls. The academy is segregated by sex, on one side of the campus is the men, and on the other is the women. There is no intermingling whatsoever. However, the weight room is in the center of campus, and it is divided by three inch thick plexiglass. On one side of the glass is the men's weight room, and on the other is the women's. The academy realized very soon after it was built that we will work harder if we are being watched by the opposite sex. All fitness classes were designed this way, but weights is the only one where you can sit and stare between sets.

Every single one of us is a virgin, and I mean EVERY single one of us, at least as far as I know. There have been some rumors about some things happening behind closed doors, but nothing with any girls that's for sure. In fact, none of us has ever even talked to a member of the opposite sex, but that doesn't mean that we aren't feeling the hormones flowing every time we see them on the other side of that glass wall, wearing their black compression capris and crimson athletic t-shirts. From the moment you enter the gym and see them across from you, you instantly perk up a little, and this goes for everyone, at least for the guys. Just the fantasy of being able to actually make human connection with one of them is enough to get us going. The promise that one day we will be able to interact with them. That is the only benefit of turning 17, it means I'm that much closer to the preseason tour for the arena, which is one step closer to the end of this segregation. I've heard that once you leave the academy you actually get to interact with them from time to time, and I can't wait for that to happen. While seeing the girls on the other side of the glass is exciting, it's equally depressing when I think about it, they are right there, and we can't even talk to them. It's human nature to want to intermingle with the opposite sex, but yet we are denied that privilege and only allowed to look at them.

Just for fun from time to time guys will do dumb stuff to show off, or entertain the girls, every now and then this will wind up in a trip to the box, but as long as you don't go too crazy the orderlies will usually allow it. Clarence and I are no exception. Every chest day we start with bench press, and every chest day we choose the bench closest to the wall. We warm-up with just the bar to get our blood flowing, but on the first rep we will make it seem as though it weighs a million pounds one way or another. This is ironic because Clarence and I are two of the best in our class for bench press. We do this gag in part for getting attention from the girls, but also because it's funny to us every time no matter how many times we do it.

Today I am up first, so I sit down on the bench and start swinging my arms back and forth before laying down as though I am trying to get super amped up to just lift the bar. When I lay down I set my arch as though I'm about to max out. Clarence is in spotting position and ready to help me with the lift off, which he does. I come down slow, then when the bar touches my chest I lift it back up about an inch and act as though I can't go any farther with it. I am holding my breath and intentionally straining so all the blood rushes to my head turning it beat red. My legs start flailing around and I drop it back down to my chest and shake my head as though I can't do it. Clarence grabs the bar as if to help me, and he acts as if the weight is too much for him to lift off my body. It is quite the spectacle, as always, and as soon as we do this I then bust out 20 reps as if it is nothing. I look through the glass when I am finished and notice that there are a few girls with smirks on their faces shaking their heads. This is a victory in my mind. Clarence and I both let out a quick laugh.

After we each do our final set on bench press and we're taking the clips off to take the weight off Clarence taps me on the shoulder, "Hey man," he says, "Your girl's here." I look over to see a girl walking in the entrance on the other side of the glass, *my girl*. She is perfect in every way, roughly 5'3" tall, dark brown hair, not like muddy brown, but so dark it's almost black. She has the deepest blue eyes, it's like looking into a bottomless hole in the ocean, so deep that once I gaze into them I feel as though I'm falling, like that feeling I get when I try and jump after doing squats. It's exhilarating, and weakening at the same time. I have no idea what her name is, but we call her Dime, because she is my perfect ten. Just seeing her

16

enter the room makes my heart rate increase, which is saying something since we are working out.

Dime and I have a relationship, at least on some level. I can't really say for sure because I don't have any experience with relationships or any relationships from which to reference, but I'm pretty sure that's what we have. I'll never forget the first time I saw her, I was six years old and waiting to spar in my hand to hand combat class. As I waited, my eyes wandered across the glass and I saw her. Everything slowed down. In that moment, I watched as she was slamming some poor girl to the ground, with an intense look of concentration across her face. The girl lay there, pinned. The moment Dime realized she had won, she stood and turned away from her victory with a smile starting to form in the corner of her mouth. Something about that moment drew me in. Something about this pretty girl on the other side of the glass with a ferocity about her, as well as satisfaction after the fact. She looked up, and was looking at me, not through me. A spark of curiosity lit her eyes, and swept its way across her face. Perhaps she was curious why I was staring, perhaps she felt drawn in just as I was, who knows? Her smile was gone so fast that I'm not sure anyone other than me saw it. That moment was mine, that smile was mine, and as the smile faded from her face, it reappeared on mine. This was the first, but not the last time we locked gazes through the glass.

The very next day in the same class I couldn't help but watch her, she looked at me part-way through the class and I smiled and waved at her like an idiot, she blushed and turned away, I was scolded by the teacher in front of the entire class. This became a regular thing, not the waving, but the staring. Time and time again I would catch myself staring across that glass looking at her, watching her. She slowly began to do the same too. Before long we would see each other as we walked in the class and smile at each other and exchange a slight nod, or a subtle wave from the hip so no one else could notice. It was like we were sending secret codes to each other, a secret language of our own that no one else knew, because if they did we would get in trouble for it. Every now and then I would make

17

funny faces when the instructor wasn't looking to make her laugh; a few times I felt bad though because her instructor noticed her laughing and got in her face about it. She never pointed me out so I could take the fall for breaking the rules though.

As time passed it was as if we had formed some sort of invisible bond that simply can't be explained. It was as if I could sense her presence whenever she was nearby. If I ever got to class before her I always knew the moment she walked into the room, and for days where she arrived first I could locate here instantly once I got to class. This connection that we had formed earned me my fair share of trips to the box on her behalf, but they were all worth it. One time about six months after we had met we were in hand to hand combat, and she got hit. Hard. It hurt me just watching it. My feet carried me over to the wall and my hand was on the glass before I even realized what I had done. Her entire class' eyes filled with shock at the sight of what I was doing, which caused her to look back at me. I smiled, and she gave a slight smile back, before here eyes switched to panic as she realized exactly what I was doing. Moments later I was whisked away to the box, but I kept smiling until I was out of the room.

Every year at the academy students move on to a new set of classes, and the people in your classes are shuffled. Usually the only constant is your roommate. Dime and I always had at least one class together. On the last day of our Seventh year as our class with each other was coming to an end I looked over at her, and she back at me. We paused and I whispered to her in that moment, "Until next time." I'm not 100% certain, but I think she understood me and said it back. Unfortunately my lip reading wasn't the greatest back then. I knew that there was a chance I wouldn't see her the next day, so I wanted to leave things on a positive moment, it's not goodbye, it's just until the next time we see each other, no matter how long that may be. From then on at the end of every class year we would repeat this process and tell each other those three words, almost like a good luck charm. For seven years it worked. However, at the end of our 13th year it lost it's power. We had known each other for eight years

18

now, and seen one another every single day over that span, this year however I was feeling overconfident and decided to take it to the next level. At the end of the class, when everyone was leaving, I walked over to the glass and put my hand on it as we locked eyes, and she did the same. "Until next time," we each whispered. Unfortunately we weren't cautious enough and we were spotted. Orderlies grabbed the two of us and pulled us away from one another. I felt terrible knowing that she was likely being taken to the box, as was I. I reached out to her and whispered "I'm sorry," she smiled and nodded as though it was okay. At the time I didn't know the full cost of what I had done, I wasn't aware that my actions would have consequences outside of an hour trip to the box.

It crushed me inside, but I started my 14th year curriculum the next day and she was no where to be found. For the first time in eight years we didn't lock eyes and exchange smiles. For the first time in what seems like forever I wasn't greeted in any of my classes by that familiar, beautiful face. There were no secret waves, no whispering "hello" to one another under our breath so no one could hear, and only we could see. It was as if a part of me had been taken away, and I didn't know how to handle it. So I didn't. I did my best not to think about her, and instead to focus more on my training. I was always a top performer, but without Dime there I started to emerge at the top of the top. I put all of my energy into training because I knew that if I thought about her it would hurt for some reason. I still caught myself looking across the glass at the start of every class, but she was never there. I started to think that she never would be again.

Two years passed, Dime had become a ghost of the past. The first day of my 16th year was upon me and I was finally given to liberty to create my own workout routine with Clarence. We entered the weight room that day ready to tear it up and separate ourselves from the pack with our own unique workouts, but as soon as we entered the gym I felt something strange. I felt a sensation that seemed familiar, but long forgotten; something I hadn't felt in a long time. In that moment I paused and looked across the glass, and there

19

she was. For the first time in two years Dime was standing opposite me. She had changed a lot over the two year span that we were apart, and came back gorgeous. She was taller, her hair longer, her physique had drastically improved to the point where she didn't even look real to me. The most beautiful girl I had ever seen had left and come back even more so. When last we saw each other we were friends, maybe even a little more than that, bonded for sure, but seeing her now my heart ached different than before. I wanted her on a whole other level. Our eyes locked and we smiled at each other. I did a subtle wave and whispered "hi" under my breath, she did the same. It didn't take Clarence long to notice what was happening and snap me out of it. He was still focused on the task at hand, but I was caught up in the moment. Since that moment not a single day has gone by where I haven't seen her face. I know that the day will come again eventually where I don't, but that's future Royce's problem.

I've read about things like love at first sight, or soul mates, and I don't know if I believe in such things, but maybe that's what this is. Or maybe it's just a fantasy that we each live in and we'll never get to actually do anything about it. I want to meet her so bad it actually hurts, after seeing her on the other side of that glass for so many years I can't wait until the day that it actually happens.

Shortly after she checks in, she looks around our side of the room, and she sees me, at least I think she sees me, it's either me or Clarence since we are the only two in the area. I smile at her, she smiles back at me and whispers hello. It feels good seeing her on my birthday, even if she doesn't know it's my birthday. I've had ample opportunities to tell her over the years, but I don't care much for birthdays so I've just kept it to myself. Come to think of it, I don't know her birthday either. Maybe she feels the same way. She and her partner, a pretty blonde that is roughly the same height, walk over to the bench press closest to us. The weight rooms mirror each other, so we are only about ten feet from each other when she sits down. "So you were saying something about doing a few more sets?" Clarence asks slyly while trying to hide a smirk.

"Actually yeah," I respond, "that's exactly what I was saying."

"Happy birthday man."

I smile and put the clips back on the bar. As I lay back down to do my set and grab the bar I look up and see Clarence looking across the glass with a confused look on his face, followed by a few awkward sideways head jerks and then he mouths something, but I can't make out the words from this angle, "What are you doing?" I ask.

"I think your girl is trying to say something to you." A grin grows across his face.

I look over at Dime, she looks around cautiously to make sure no one is paying attention then she whispers what looks like "happy birthday," puts her hand up to her mouth and blows me a kiss and winks at me before returning to her workout.

I

Am

On

Cloud

Nine

I freeze, I am overwhelmed with so much emotion and desire and shock at the same time, I can feel my face turning red with the huge pathetic grin I have from ear to ear. We have always exchanged glances, smiles, waves, even hand touches across the glass, but never has she blown me a kiss before. This is officially the best birthday ever. Clarence claps his hands together really quick and jumps up in the air "YES!" He says ecstatically as he giggles like a school girl. He then notices that he's making a scene. An orderly is staring so he regains as much composure as possible and asks, "Best birthday present ever or what?" A huge smile covers his face.

"Did you tell her to do that?"

"I mean, I might've hinted that it's your birthday."

"Its times like these that I remember why I like having you as a bunkmate," I say. My day is officially made, and no matter what happens that will be all I can think about for the rest of the day. Dime blew a kiss at me, at ME, and I didn't even get in trouble for it. This is easily the highlight of my day/week/month/year/life.

The rest of the workout is pretty routine. After weights we walk back to our room and grab towels to go shower. The academy uses community showers. One for each floor of the dorms. After we shower we change into our casual uniforms, crimson polo shirts with black kakis, socks, shoes, and belts. We have our Learn Smart sessions for the next couple of hours before lunch and then our combat training classes. The only thing we say to each other during all of this is just the same few words over and over. I say "Cloud nine man," and he responds "You're welcome." And we both smile and continue on.

Learn Smart sessions are spent in a cubical with a headset that covers your eyes and has noise cancelling headphones. Over 100 years ago they developed a computer application that would stream words from text in front of you one word at a time. It is designed to allow the reader to process information at speeds greater than they would be able to read on their own. It starts at 250 words per minute when you are young, but by the time you turn 12 you are reading 1,000 words per minute and retaining all of the information you are presented. Many topics, such as geology, will have pictures attached as well. Pictures stay on the screen for a few seconds so you can take it in. Every week we are required to cover certain amounts of content and we are then tested over it to ensure retention. If you pass you move on, if not it is presented to you again until you do pass. I've never had to retake a section.

Every week is something new, the main purpose behind these Learn Smarts is to provide us with a high school equivalent education, as well as to educate us about everything in the outside world. We even learn about the more unsettling topics such as drug users, gangs, sex, and abuse. The idea is that, should we win our freedom, we'll be prepared for most of the situations we may encounter if we choose to leave. The first thing you cover every week is a review of arena origin, the events that led to its creation, and the reasoning behind it, as well as why it is a gift to us. The academy teaches us that if it weren't for The Arena most, if not all, of us would have been aborted. Thanks to the show we are given 18 years of life, and a shot at freedom should we earn it. Even if you manage to take nothing from the Learn Smarts, they want you to have a thorough understanding of why the arena exists. Today is my arena refresher, afterwards I am supposed to cover human anatomy and physiology.

Clarence and I arrive at the Learn Smart zone and sit down at our respective cubicles. I grab my headset, put it on, and power it up. The retinal scan for Learn Smarts is done through the headset. Once I am identified it goes right into my lesson.

This is the gist of what we have to read every week:

The Earth was estimated to be able to support between nine and ten billion people, in the year 2050 we reached nine billion, by the year 2100 it had risen to over ten billion.

Overcrowding was becoming a serious concern. In the year 2120 the Earth's population reached 11 billion. The UN held a meeting to address its growing concern about population. Scientists explained that we had to act in order to reduce population or face dire consequences. Previous measures that proved effective at keeping the population in check were no longer factors. There was no more war since the last of the oil reserves had been depleted by 2087, and foreign affairs amongst countries had drastically improved since then with the transition to alternative energy sources. Disease was no longer a factor with modern medicine, there was a vaccine or treatment for virtually every pathogen known to man. Also, the average life expectancy had risen to 95 years, an all-time high.

Essentially, people were reproducing, but no one was dying, and thus causing overcrowding. The government tried to compensate through vertical farming, as well as the use of skyscraper apartment complexes, but it just wasn't enough.

Something had to be done.

In 2021 the Earth's leaders decided on a new set of rules for reproduction. All males would receive mandatory vasectomies at the age of 13. These procedures could be reversed upon the male turning 18 so long as they managed to pass an IQ test with a score over 100, since it was the average, and managed to maintain a body fat percentage under 25%. The idea was that this would prevent many people from reproducing, and those who were allowed would be passing on good genes. Regular physicals would be done every six months for the rest of their lives to ensure maintenance of these standards, should the male no longer qualify the vasectomy would be done again.

The next measure of population control that was enacted was that no female should be permitted to have more than two children, since two children per couple is just enough to replace them. Should a female get pregnant with a third child, a fine of 100,000 dollars would be charged to them should they decide to have the child rather than aborting it. This was roughly a year's income for those riding the poverty line, so the vast majority of people couldn't afford it.

Scientists projected that these two means of population control would greatly reduce the rate by which the population was increasing, but it still didn't solve the overcrowding factor. It wasn't until 2122 that a man by the name of Gustav Black approached the UN with an idea to help. His idea was a game show of sorts, except in this game the winner would be the only man left alive. The UN was reluctant at first, but before long Mr. Black had permission to start preparations for The Arena.

At first it started as a show for anyone who wanted to participate, the prize was 75,000 dollars to the victor of a one on one combat match. The show was an instant hit. By 2123 it was the number one show in the world, with arenas in every major country across the globe. It quickly diversified its competitions as well. Before long, there were two on two matches (doubles), female matches, and even intersex doubles matches. Eventually the crowds grew hungry for more intense matches however, which presented Mr. Black with a problem. People were growing weary of seeing amateurs make idiots out of themselves. In a fight to the death, people wanted to see professionals go at it. In 2125 he found his solution, and the Arena Academy was founded. Mr. Black would offer to pay 150,000 dollars to the family expecting a third child in order to cover the fee and provide extra finances in exchange for the parents agreeing to give the child to the Academy. Getting permission from the government was easy enough, he simply proposed it as a way to further stimulate the economy, as well as a gift of life to those who would otherwise be aborted.

The amount of children being sold to the academy was astonishing, most every would-be abortion of the lower class quickly turned to selling their child to the academy. Once in the academy children would be looked after until they turned 18, at which time they would fight in the arena. Mr. Black established that these children owed a debt to the Academy for the $150,000 paid to get them, as well as an additional $100,000 for every year they resided at there. It was a great way to give third born children a chance at life. These children are allowed to be born into the family of the Academy where they are taken care of and trained for the honor of fighting in The Arena. While at the academy all children receive a proper education, are well fed, clothed, and provided with excellent skills to fight. Upon turning 18, they will receive $100,000 dollars for every match they win, which means that they would have to win only 20 matches to settle their debt with the academy and earn their freedom.

By the year 2143 the first children were coming of age, and then the real fighting began. The Arena is the number one show on television, it is on seven days a week, and the stadium that it is hosted in sells out every single day. Each day starts with amateur matches to get the crowd riled up, followed by at least one match of every type involving academy students. Every season starts off with a marathon, in which dozens of matches take place every day for the first week of the season. Day one of a new season has no amateur matches, instead it starts with two of the top contenders and ends with another two from their respective match types (male/female singles/doubles). Students can fight as often as they want, but are required to participate in at least one match every month barring injury. Should they be injured they are allowed time to recover, however should the injury be self-inflicted no such allowance is given.

Many will go on to win their freedom, but countless will die trying. Should these students fail to earn their freedom in the first year, an additional $100,000 is tacked on to their debt. Some manage to win their freedom inside of a year, others take almost two years, and a select few take longer than that due to injuries and special circumstances, such as a doubles partner dying. Once their debt is settled, students are given any excess prize money they are due in excess of their debt and allowed to leave the Academy, should they choose. Many stay and continue to fight when necessary in order to pay their dues at the Academy. One of the best fighters to date, Roman 2127 won 120 matches in order to pay for himself to be able to live the rest of his life at the Academy.

Over the years many other game shows have come and gone with similar concepts to The Arena, but none can match its popularity. It is a very dark concept, with dire consequences for the losers of every episode, but it is deemed a necessary evil, and continues to thrive after 32 years.

I hate Learn Smart. It's boring, but it's required. If you refuse to do your Learn Smarts you are tied to a chair and your eyes are taped open while they stream that day's lesson, and then you go to the box. No thanks. After we finish our Learn Smarts Clarence and I meet up and head for the cafeteria. Lunch time. My brain feels a little fried, but I am still on cloud nine. All that is left in my day is lunch, combat precision training, cardio, yoga, and dinner.

"Man," Clarence starts, "I can't stand Learn Smart, most boring part of the day every day." I am with him on that, but it's still a good day for me.

I just throw my arms up in the air and declare "CLOUD NINE!"

"You're welcome," Clarence says in between laughs.

"Seriously though man, I really appreciate what you did, you could have been sent to the box for a stunt like that, even if you were subtle about it."

"Nah man, I knew I was good, it wasn't that bad, and even if I did go to the box for a bit it would be worth it. It's your birthday, and you should enjoy it." Sometimes I wonder how I managed to get paired up with someone as great as Clarence.

We get to the cafeteria, get in line, get scanned, receive our trays, and sit down at an empty table. I'm not sure how, but Joseph and Gordon never show up before us, for any meals. We are almost finished eating when they finally do make an appearance. "Mmmm, smells delightful," Gordon says as he sits down.

"Birthday going good so far Royce?" Joseph asks.

"You could say that," I say with a grin.

"My boy Royce here got a little something special in weights today," Clarence explains.

"Oh really?" Gordon asks, "What was it? Special groin massage from the orderlies perhaps?"
"Even better," Clarence says, "Dime blew him a kiss!"

"Don't lie," Gordon responds, his eyes squint in disbelief.

"Yeah I have to say I'm reluctant to believe you," Joseph states with a raised brow.

"It's true!" Clarence declares with excitement, "I hinted over to her that it was his birthday, and when the orderlies weren't looking she blew him a kiss and winked at him! My boy has some mad game with the ladies. Today it was just blowing a kiss, but who knows in a couple months it could be something a little more once our season gets going, if you know what I mean." Clarence elbows me with a huge smile on his face.

"Yeah yeah," I say, "we'll see, but I'm not gonna get my hopes up. The kiss was enough for me for now."

"Good for you Royce," Joseph says, "everyone deserves something special on their birthday."

"Ooh, I'm Royce," Gordon says mockingly with his hands by his face and his eyes crossed, "and I gotted a kiss from a girly on da udder side of da glass, look at me, I is a special boy."

"More than you've ever gotten," Clarence replies.

"BURN!" Joseph says as we all started to laugh.

"Besides," I say, "it wasn't just a kiss, she winked too. So I've got that going for me, which is nice."

"Haha okay then," Gordon says, "let me know how that wink works out for you. Ahem, yes mister orderly, I would like to have your finest delicacies for lunch today please, for you see a cute girl winked at me today. I'm kind of a big deal around these parts you see."

"Okay, jerk," I say. I'm pretty sure it's impossible to be on the winning side of a conversation/debate with Gordon. He always manages to take it to the next level or get the last word. Sometimes it's funny, even if it's at the expense of another, but other times it's just annoying. I feel a little bad for thinking about it from time to time, but I honestly don't know if we would be friends with Gordon if it weren't for Joseph.

Joseph, Clarence and I have been friends since we met Joseph when we were seven and had a conditioning class together. I can still remember the first day we met him, the majority of the class had just finished running three miles and were keeling over from exhaustion, all but Joseph. Joseph finished his run right after us, he then turned around and even though his face was flushed, body drenched in sweat, and he looked like he might pass out, he still managed to stand up and cheer on the last few kids who hadn't finished yet. Even though he was just as exhausted as we were he managed to stand up and smile like it didn't even bother him. I knew right then that I wanted to be friends with him. I asked him afterwards why he did that, and he said, "Because everyone likes to be cheered on, and we don't get that enough here, especially the kids who just aren't that good. So if I can make someone feel a little better just by doing something as simple and cheering for them and telling them they are doing great, why wouldn't I? Everyone deserves to feel good about themselves regardless of if they finished first or last, so long as they did their best and they finished. If it was up to me no one would ever have to feel bad here." As he was telling me this the kids who finished in the bottom five were being chastised by the instructor. Joseph had such a unique outlook on life from such a young age, all we ever got was negative reinforcement for underperforming, the only time we would get any sort of encouragement was if we finished first.

"I like that," was all I could say in response as I nodded my head and squinted slightly while trying to process the concept of trying to make everyone happy. Clarence then proceeded to invite him to sit by us at lunch, and the rest is history. I think part of the reason that I was so drawn to Joseph from the get go is because he reminded me so much of Lawrence. Both of them were kind souls, the only difference is that Joseph managed to assimilate where Lawrence could not.

It wasn't until Gordon became his roommate that he joined our crew, and he was even more jaded then than he is now. I don't know what it was, maybe it was that he just felt alone so he always had to lash out at others. We didn't really like him, but we tolerated him because of Joseph. I think having Joseph as a roommate was good for Gordon though, Joseph is basically the yin to Gordon's yang. He brings light where Gordon throws darkness. It's helped Gordon lighten up a bit over the years, he's still a jerk though. You could say that Gordon grows on you eventually, but it's not the type of growth you necessarily want, more like an unexpected mold or fungus that you can't do anything about. We still love him though, but its a weird kind of love, like a love for a brother that you aren't about to tell everyone you're related to, but ultimately you're there for him if he needs you.

I asked Joseph why he kept hanging out with Gordon a couple of weeks after they became roommates. And in true Joseph fashion, he said, "I know he may seem a little rough around the edges, but he's had it tough. His roommate committed suicide, and he found the body when he was going to change between classes. Seeing something like that has an impact, not to mention he didn't have any other friends besides him. I've had you guys for a few years now, and I can't imagine what it would be like to lose the only person I have to hang on to. How are you supposed to act if you lose the only thing keeping you grounded? I know he's spiraling a little bit now, but deep down he's a great guy with a big heart. He just has a hard time letting anyone in that's all. And he's not like this all the time, whenever it's just us in the dorm room, especially at night, he's just a normal guy, and his disruptive exterior fades away. Plus you know me, I don't want anyone to have to hurt or feel bad if there's anything I can do to help, and with him there is and I can, so I do." Hearing Joseph talk about Gordon that way helped shine some light on why he is the way he is, it doesn't change the fact that he's a little much, but it helps me even today to tolerate him when he's pushing my buttons. I don't know what I would have done if I were in his shoes, maybe I would have become disruptive just like him.

Clarence and I have finished eating at this point, and the lunch hour is almost up. Combat precision training is our next class, and it's on the other side of campus. We say our goodbyes and clear our trays, and then head back to our dorm room to change uniforms yet again. Our combat training uniforms are compression clothing, black compression shorts with sleeveless crimson compression shirts. Our shoes are the same as our gym shoes. Luckily this will be the last time we have to change clothes, the rest of the day we can just wear these uniforms if we want. Even though they are the most ridiculous looking uniforms, it's too much of a hassle to have to go back and change again.

Once Clarence and I get to class we will have to part ways, the reason it is called precision training is because it is specialized to you in what your weapon of choice will be in the arena. You are introduced to all weapons until you are 14, at which time you have to choose one to specialize in. Usually by that point you have a clear favorite, so choosing is easy. My weapon of choice is the spear, I like its versatility with regards to offense and defense as well as the option of melee or ranged combat. Clarence likes to be a "man's man" as he calls it and dual wields two swords. His favorite are scimitars, which I think is just because they look cool, but he is proficient with most every sword.

Since we have different specialties Clarence and I split upon arriving, I go to my room, and he his. Today is projectile deflection training. In the arena any and all medieval weapons are allowed, which includes bows and crossbows. The training room is the size of a football field with a track around it. The floor is a firm black rubber mat, with a red rubber track around the outside. All weapons are kept on the wall nearest the entrance, weapons at the academy are non-lethal. Most are made of wood and dull, but they are weighted accordingly to ensure you won't be thrown off by any changes when you enter the Arena and start using the real weapons.

I am one of sixty spear specialists in my class, but only six train during the same time as me. It isn't the most popular choice amongst my class, or any class for that matter. Classes are split up based on age, those turning the same age between January 1st and December 31st fall into the same class. I'm not sure why it is unpopular though, it has so much utility that in my mind it is just the hands down best pick. We start off the class with the usual warm-up, jog two laps around the track, some dynamic stretching, and another lap with our weapons. The other five students in my class run with just their spears. I have a dual specialization with spear and shield so I do my warm-up with both. Everyone thinks I am dumb for using a shield, but when push comes to shove it's easier to block arrows and knock someone over with a shield than it is with a spear alone.

"Line up!" A voice yells from near the entrance, it's our instructor Mr. Arnold. Standing 5'9" tall, with black hair, dark blue eyes and perfectly trimmed short black beard, along with a physique to match any one of us and then some; he is a very intimidating man. He has a glare that he will give us if we ever mess up that will pierce straight to your bones, maybe even your soul. We call him Mr. Arnold because he was one of the original students here, his original name was Arnold 2126, and Mr. 2126 sounded weird so he has us call him Mr. Arnold. Like me, he specialized in spears when the academy first started, he is one of the only combatants to win 20 matches in a row without ever being injured. Once he had won his freedom the academy offered him a job as an instructor, and he took it. At only 28 Mr. Arnold is experienced and wise well beyond his years, he is essentially my role model. "Single file! Deflection drill! We will start with one arrow, then progress to two, three, all the way up to 10. Then we will switch to arrows from multiple points of origin. For every arrow that hits you, you will do 100 push-ups." Mr. Arnold is strict, but effective.

We all line up as he says that the arrows being fired at us are non-lethal with blunt, soft, heads. They still hurt and leave a bruise if they hit you though. The first time we did this drill I had to do 150 pushups, and that was when he only made you do ten for each arrow that hit you. I am last in line, for this drill I am only allowed to use my spear like everyone else. We have done this drill so many times that the first part was easy, pure reaction. No one got hit for the first ten rounds. It gets a lot harder when arrows start coming from multiple places at the same time. Some people will try to do a pinwheel with their spear to deflect them, but that isn't always 100% reliable. I usually just do my best to keep moving and dodge them that way. I will deflect any that I can, but it is easier to just dodge them whenever possible in my opinion. For every round that we pass Mr. Arnold will add another archer point, we manage to make it through the first five rounds before someone gets hit. Jeffrey, a 5'6" blonde with green eyes, got hit in the thigh. There's 100 pushups. In the 7th round George, a 5"8" brown haired guy took one in the finger, he was using the pinwheel technique and it hit him right on the tip of his finger as he was spinning it. Sucks, but it's still 100 pushups.

"Tenth and final round," Mr. Arnold says after the first nine rounds are completed, "There will be no rest, there will be 10 archer points, and it will be last man standing doesn't have to do pushups. First one out will have 500, second 400, and so on." I hate it when he does this, we literally run in circles dodging arrows until five of us take an arrow. It's not so bad at the start because it's a relatively slow pace, but by the time it gets down to the final two or three of us it's exhausting.

Jeffrey is first out, followed shortly after by Billy, then George, then Stephen. Finally it is down to just me and Scott, a 6'2" crew cut brown hair brown eyes jerk that I love to hate. There is no one else here that I want to beat more than him, he is such a stiff and a stickler with the rules it's ridiculously annoying. We are literally running back and forth between the start point and the front of the line, both of us are starting to fatigue. I feel like death, my lungs are on fire, my arms are ready to fall off, and my calves are about to rip out of my skin, but I am NOT going to lose to him. There is no way I can lose, I am too strong, too determined, too committed, too- I feel a sharp pain in my ribs and it's over. I lost.

I collapse as soon as I know it is over and lay there for a second trying to catch my breath, I look over at Scott and he has his hand out to shake mine. I do it, but I don't enjoy it. "Well fought," Scott says. Jerk. At this point I would have rather just been first out and done the 500 pushups, it would have been easier.

"Royce I believe you owe me some pushups," Mr. Arnold says, "get to it." It takes everything I have, but I roll over and do them. We aren't allowed to pause between pushups for rest either, if we do we have to tack on another 50, and naturally any fuss or refusal will wind up in a trip to the box. It is only 100 though, so I manage. "Good work today everyone, see you tomorrow," and with that Mr. Arnold is gone. He isn't one to stay after class and talk, part of me wonders if that's because he doesn't want to get attached to students that will likely die in the arena.

I lay on the ground for a few minutes before getting up, everyone else has already left to go to their next classes. When I regain my composure I walk out to find Clarence waiting for me. He doesn't even look sweaty, whereas I imagine I look as bad as I feel. "Looks like you had fun," Clarence say as I am walking out.

"Loads," I respond, "carry me?"

"Yeah right, as if I want your sweat and grossness touchin' me. Cardio is going to be fun for you, I can already tell."

"I'm in no rush to get there." Cardio class is literally just an hour of running around a track, three days a week we do sprints in conjunction with it, but today is just show up and run for an hour. The track is located two floors above where we are, so we walk over to the stairs and take our time walking up. We walk through the door and scan in. The one perk of this class is that like the gym it has two tracks separated by plexiglass. I feel better as soon as we walk in. Upon entering you are required to grab a watch that tracks heart rate and speed, if you ever drop below 10mph for longer than ten seconds it starts beeping obnoxiously loud, they don't do anything to you if you do, but everyone else running hates you. The reason for the ten

34

second allowance is so that you can stop for quick hydration breaks when needed.

Clarence I start running laps together. After running six or so laps I look over and notice that Dime is running on the other track. I feel amazing, it's hard not to when you see your crush running around in a sports bra and spandex short shorts. "Slow down speedy," Clarence says, "What's gotten into you?" Then he follows my gaze and sees Dime. "Oh, well still, slow down!" I wasn't aware I was running that much faster, so I did as he said and slowed down. The rest of the hour I just kept glancing over at Dime, and I caught her looking back at me a lot too. The hour seemed to fly by, it was too fast. Even though running is relatively miserable, I would do just about anything to just be able to see Dime for as long as possible. Someday I will be able to do more than just stare, someday.

Clarence and I grab some water on the way out, and then we are off to yoga. "You're lucky it's your birthday or I would have to beat you for making me run faster out there." he complains.

"Sorry man, I didn't realize I was doing it until you said something, my bad."

"Just don't do it again, please and thank you."

"Sure thing." Yoga is a short walk, when we get there we check in and grab a mat, then we find a spot. We take our shoes and socks off and sit waiting for it to begin. Yoga is nice, but also annoying. An hour of stretching while listening to music that makes you want to fall asleep in a dim lit room gets old after doing it every day for 17 years. Every now and then someone will fall asleep in the middle of it, if they catch you they send you to the cardio room and make you do sprints, and then you go to the box. Luckily I've never gotten to that point. It's also annoying that it is the same every day, warrior one, two, and three, downward facing dog, all of the hits. If cardio went by fast, yoga takes an eternity, but once it is over we are free for the rest of the day, aside from dinner.

Clarence and I walk out and head back to our dorm. We hit the showers yet again and change back into our regular uniforms. Then we head for dinner. Super food again, oh joy. We do our scan, grab our trays, sit at an empty table, and eat. Of course it isn't long before Joseph and Gordon show up. "Dang girl you workout?" Gordon jokes as he sits down. The two of them are still in their weights uniforms, they are usually too lazy to shower before coming to dinner.

"Have fun in weights today?" Clarence asks.

"It was alright," Joseph says, "why do you ask?"

"Because you must have been just goofing around, since there's no way you two got those baby biceps lifting hard seven days a week." I almost choke on my food when he says that.

"Ouch man," Gordon says, "did you at least bring us some ice to apply to that burn? And besides, not everyone here does steroids like you two."

"You mean not everyone knows how to work hard like us," Clarence smirks. "You wish you had muscles like these." He proceeds to flex his arms at Gordon.

"Well yeah," Gordon says, "but I want my goods to still work when I get to use them."

"Like you will ever use it," I say. Joseph even laughs at that one.

"Never mind the ice," Joseph says, "he's going to need therapeutic burn cream for that one. Might even need to call a doctor to check him out." For the first time in a long time Gordon is silent for a second, he is actually at a loss for words, this really is a good birthday.

"Shut up," Gordon replies.

"Nice comeback," Clarence responds, "did you come up with that all on your own or did you need help?"

"Dime helped me come up with it actually," He says, "she's actually great at coming up with things on the spot." *Jerk*.

"Dude really," Clarence says, "he still has a few hours left of his birthday, no low blows. Besides someone like her wouldn't wipe her butt with someone like you, let alone actually talk to you."

"Yeah sure whatever," Gordon says. There is an awkward tension as we finish eating, Gordon is upset and decides to be a downer, oh well. Just Gordon being Gordon. At least he's not like he used to be. Back when he first started hanging out with us, if we ever made fun of him too much he would just lose it and storm off. At least now he can take the abuse like a man, he just sulks a little sometimes. You have to be able to take it if you're going to dish it out all the time.

Clarence and I finish eating and say our goodbyes before clearing our trays and heading back to our dorms. We spend the rest of the night just watching television in our dorm room, we are only allowed to watch reruns of The Arena, but it is better than nothing, and good for studying. I am not in the mood for much else. Some people use this time to work on their weapons training, or their hand to hand combat, but it is my birthday and I want to be lazy. Clarence is totally on board for that, it may not be a true day off, but six hours of nothingness is as close as it gets for us. The only other thing we do is brush our teeth before bed.

As I lay in bed, and look back at my day I am pretty happy overall. I hit the weights hard, witnessed Gordon being speechless, and had a moment with Dime. The only thing that could have made the day better is if I beat Scott in combat precision training, but hey I can't expect everything to go my way. It was a good day, one of the best days I've ever had. Like I said I'm not too big on birthdays, they are usually more depressing than they are exciting, but this one was actually pretty good. With luck I will be able to return to my paradise. Never having been outside is a depressing feeling, to have to read about it and see pictures in my Learn Smarts only makes me want it more. Someday I will venture outside, someday I will find that grassy plain and lay beneath the sun, someday I will rid myself of this wretched place and finally find peace.

Once I fall asleep I manage to get back to my paradise. The only thing that changes is that this time I am not alone. I thought that total solitude was the ideal heaven for me, but tonight I realized that I was wrong. Tonight I share the grassy plain with Dime. Neither of us talks, we just lie there, staring at each other, soaking up the sun and listening to the breeze blow by.

II

Time passes, and my routine remains the same day in and day out. Wake up, breakfast, weights, Learn Smart, lunch, combat precision training, cardio, yoga, dinner. Every day is the same, with slight differences in conversation and topics/routines within the classes. Twice a week Clarence and I go practice our hand to hand combat, and every night we watch The Arena on TV, we aren't watching it because we enjoy it, but rather as a study guide. We use the show as a way of seeing what to expect once we get out there and do it ourselves. We pay attention to everything, because every match whether it be singles or doubles is relevant since we don't know where we will wind up yet. You aren't told which category you will be in until three months before you start, on your preseason tour. I still see Dime every day, she doesn't blow me any more kisses though, or really act different than she did before. It's like it never happened, sometimes it feels like it was a dream, but it wasn't. She may not think about it much, but I know I do.

Seasons in The Arena are divided up into three month segments, everyone who turns 18 within a given three month segment will be the new contestants for the following three months. For Clarence and I, we'll be in the segment between January 1st and March 31st. Joseph and Gordon are in the tail end of that segment as well, with their birthdays in March.

Nights are becoming progressively more restless for me, some nights I am in the plains with Dime, other nights I'm in the arena. Night Terrors are common in the academy, especially amongst those over 17. Some nights it's so bad that I wake violently and jump off my bunk with my heart pounding as though I am ready to fight. "Go back to sleep," Clarence will say, "just a dream man." Clarence doesn't have the same problem, he is calm and collected even when he sleeps. I wish I could be so confident, I'm ready, but somewhere deep down I don't know that I really am.

Six months finally passes, and for once I wake up in a good mood right from the start. I'm even up before the wake-up call. "You feelin' alright?" Clarence asks when he sees me sit up five minutes early.

"I'm great, today I finally get to eat something other than paste." Today marks the day that I finally get to eat good food, at least I imagine it's good. Clarence had gotten his two weeks ago, and it smelled amazing. Just sitting next to him while he ate it was enough to cause a slight sensation of euphoria in my nostrils. When you get upgraded to real food you aren't allowed to share sadly, and if you are caught sharing it with anyone you are put right back on super food until you go on tour.

"I don't know what you are so excited about," Clarence says, "I mean it's only the most delicious food you've ever experienced. It's just an instant mouthgasm as soon as it touches your tongue. It's only one of the most pleasurable experiences you'll have had to date. No big deal man." Clarence thinks he's funny, but I'm starving. My stomach knows what's coming and it can't wait either.

I change in no time and am ready to go, for the first time ever I am actually waiting on Clarence to be ready, and he is taking his sweet time too. I can tell he's slower than usual, he is enjoying torturing me. "Hurry up!" I yell.

"Calm down man," he responds, "you can't rush perfection."

"I can, and I will. When you got your first meal you dragged me out of bed extra early." He literally grabbed me and pulled me out of bed, I woke as I was falling to the ground.

Clarence finally finishes getting ready after what feels like an eternity, it's five minutes past wake-up call. "Well what are you waiting for? Let's go slowness."

"Jerk," I say as I rush out the door, he laughs.

All that is going through my head as we walk over, and as we wait in line is *food food food food food food*. I feel like a drug addict looking to score, and I haven't even tried the drugs is the sad part, I have only seen other people using them. The line is so long it's depressing, at least it feels that way. Really it is the same as usual, maybe slightly smaller since we are a couple minutes earlier than usual.

Finally the time comes, time to scan. I step up, get scanned, and in front of me appears the most beautiful sight possible. A tray of real food. It may possibly be the most beautiful thing I've ever seen, at least it is in this moment, Dime still has food beat when I'm thinking rationally. It looks amazing, just like the pictures in Lean Smart, skim milk, a fruit bowl of orange, banana, and strawberry slices as well as grapes, small bowl of low-fat honey Greek yogurt,

40

and finally to top it off two plump chicken breasts. I grab the tray and rush over to the nearest empty table, leaving Clarence behind. After I sit down I close my eyes and breathe in the smell of the chicken, my mouth quivers in anticipation.

Once I'm satisfied that I have waited long enough I grab one of the grapes and set it gently on my tongue before biting into it, ever so slowly. An explosion of flavor fills my mouth. I let it sit there as I absorb the mind blowing taste as I chew, so sweet and tart. *Amazing.* Next I take a spoonful of yogurt. As the yogurt touches my tongue I close my eyes and let it rest there for a moment. It's so sweet and bitter and exotic, so good. After the brief pause I slowly drag the spoon across my tongue and out of my mouth, making sure I get every speck of yogurt possible. Now it's time for the chicken, the blend of whatever seasoning they put on it only makes it better, it's somewhat salty and bland, but delicious all the same. Feeling the warmth in my mouth as I chew, the tender moist chicken radiates heat throughout my mouth and I feel it warming my throat and stomach as I swallow each bite. The warmth alone is a new experience, it's so relaxing that the combination of sensations I'm experiencing is entrancing. After sampling all of the food I essentially inhale it, it's gone in seconds. Finally I wash it down with the milk, which is slightly thicker than water. I let it swish around in my mouth for a few moments before swallowing in order to take in the flavor. I feel the temperature of the milk change from cold to warm as it sits in my mouth. Everything is delicious.

"Wow," Clarence says, "did you even taste it?"

"At first," I say as I set my empty milk bottle carton down, "today is going to be a good day."

"Haha, alright then," Clarence responds.

"You seriously already ate it all?" Gordon says with a furrowed brow as he and Joseph sit down. "Talk about selfish."

"Selfish?" I ask.

"Yeah," he responds, "selfish. You should know that you are supposed to wait for me to get a few good smells in before you eat it so I can fantasize about what it will be like when it's my turn."

"My bad," I say, "I'll be sure to be more considerate of your needs from now on."

"That's right you will, or else." He crosses his arms and throws his head back, nose up to the side.

"Or else what?"

"Haven't figured that out yet, but it would be bad that's for sure."

"So how was it?" Joseph asks.

"I doubt he can tell you," Clarence says. "He ate it so fast I don't think he knows what any of it tasted like."

"What a waste," Gordon says.

"It was great," I say, "I savored the first few bites, then devoured it because it was so good."

"Man I can't wait," Joseph says as he leans back and puts his hands behind his head with his eyes closed and a smile from ear to ear, "just a few more weeks."

Every meal from now on is real food, and every time it's amazing. The best part is the variety that they give us. Some days we have chicken, other times its steak, I get to try all sorts of sea food too - which is by far the best in my opinion. Sushi is easily my favorite, Learn Smart made it look and sound gross, but I love it. I only get it a few times, but every time I have it I jump up and down like an idiot that just won the lottery. I also get to try various pastas, oatmeal, rice, various fruits and vegetables. Meals become a means to be excited rather than depressed as it were before. Sadly the food can't cover up what's coming, as more time passes the arena is drawing closer and closer.

In the academy we don't celebrate holidays, but we are aware of them through our Learn Smarts. When January comes around Gordon decides to make a toast at breakfast. "Happy New Year's everyone, I know it's a little late, but we aren't exactly able to stay up past curfew to really celebrate, so I'd like to make a toast now."

"You serious?" Clarence asks.

"Yes," Gordon responds, "now everyone raise a glass, or carton of milk for that matter." We all laugh a little, but we go along with it. "Here's to us, we've come this far, and the road is going to get very bumpy, very soon. So Happy New Year's, it may be the last one we are guaranteed, but I'll be damned if it's the last one we have together."

"CHEERS!" We all say in unison as we tap our milk cartons together. This is easily one of the most cheerfully depressing moments I have ever experienced, it makes me think about how I might not have my friends sitting with me a year from now. By this time next year the odds of any of us being alive is slim, and the odds of all of us being here is microscopic, but it feels nice to have a joyful and hopeful moment with my friends. It sucks to think about, but this will likely be one of the last truly happy moments I share with all of them.

Just over two weeks later Clarence turns 18, it's a hard day. You don't fight right when you turn 18, you have until the next season starts for the show, but it's a symbolic moment that means your battle for survival will be starting very soon. Two weeks after his birthday it's my turn. I don't let it phase me, I knew it was coming so I just treat it like I would any other day. My birthday is a milestone however, it means we have exactly two months until the preseason tour. It also means we have two months until they tell us whether we will be fighting singles or doubles. It seems like all of the days are starting to blur together now, the last month at the academy is going by faster than all of the others, as if time is picking up speed the closer the arena gets.

The morning of April 1st feels strange. I wake up totally calm and collected, knowing today is the start of the preseason. The wakeup call comes just as it always does, but this time it is followed with a knock at our door. Clarence opens the door to see one of the orderlies standing there. "Be ready to leave in twenty minutes," the orderly says, "breakfast will be served on the train, wear your regular uniforms." He moves on to the next room. Today is the day, everyone at the academy turning 18 between January 1st and March 31st will be leaving for the preseason. It doesn't feel real. I don't want it to be real. Sadly, it is.

"You ready for this?" Clarence asks me.

"Nope, but that doesn't mean it isn't going to happen anyways."

I get up and take a quick shower since we won't be doing weights this morning. I put on my regular uniform, khakis and red polo shirt. The orderly didn't give us directions where to go, but that's because we already know. There is only one exit to the academy, and every three months we see a line of students exit through it. Clarence and I don't speak to each other on the walk over, we're both nervous. I feel my hands start shaking as we get closer. I've never been outside the academy before, not since I was an infant. For Clarence, he hasn't been outside the academy since being brought here as a young boy. As we near the exit we are met by a huge line of students. I see Gordon and Joseph standing towards the front, which is weird since they are always late to the cafeteria. Gordon looks back and sees us, so he flexes and makes tough guy faces at us, followed by shallow laughter, there is no stopping that guy from making a spectacle of himself. I shake my head, but can't help but smile a little. Joseph looks at us and smiles, but this smile is different than his usual smile. There is something missing, it doesn't have the same feeling it usually does. Joseph must be on edge as well.

After waiting in line for a few minutes it seems as though everyone has showed up, but it's hard to tell by how many people

44

are here, there has to be at least 1000 people in line with us, it seems endless. All of the sudden I hear a noise from the front of the line, I look to see the two huge metal doors start to slide open. None of us have any idea what lies on the other side of those doors, I feel both scared and excited.

To my surprise once the doors are opened I don't see the outside world, instead I see a train terminal. Apparently the only way in or out of the academy is by train? I was so excited at the possibility of seeing the sky, maybe even a sunrise for the first time, and now that excitement is replaced with longing and anger. An orderly stands in the doorway with a scanner set up on either side of him. "Scan yourself in and go to the seat the computer assigns you." He shouts loud enough for everyone to hear.

The line moves pretty quickly, it only takes a few seconds for each student to scan and read their seat assignment. It's only about 5 minutes before Clarence and I scan in. Clarence goes first and is assigned to seat 121, I do my scan and get 122. "Man, I have to sit next to some loser," I say trying to lighten the mood.

"Yeah I know the feeling," We both laugh half-heartedly.

We enter the train and find our seats, once we're seated we wait for a good 20 minutes before we finally hear the train doors shut. Shortly after the doors shut we hear the intercom come on, "Greetings students," a male voice says, "as I'm sure you are all aware, this marks the start of the spring preseason, leading up to the spring season of The Arena. Provided in the pockets located in the back of the seat in front of you are your assignments. You have all been divided up into singles or doubles and put into a battle group. We will soon be departing for New York City, it will be roughly a six hour trip. Upon arrival we will provide you with further instructions as to where you will be going and what will be expected of you. Breakfast will be served shortly, lunch will be served roughly an hour before our arrival, enjoy." And with that the intercom shut off and I feel the train start to move slowly.

45

Clarence and I each reach for our respective assignments, they are in sealed envelopes with our names on them. "You go first," Clarence says.

"Hell no, you go first."

"Same time?"

"Okay, I guess if you really want to you can go first."

"Whatever man," he says as he rips the top of his envelope and pulls out a sheet of paper. "Clarence 2137," he reads aloud, "date of birth January 16th 2137. We here by congratulate you on your completion of your training at the academy, and wish you luck in the arena. You have been assigned to participate in the doubles category. This means you will take place in two on two combat, your partner for which shall be ROYCE 2137! YEAH BABY! WOOOOOOOO!" he shouts. I can't believe it.

"Are you serious!? You better not be messing with me or I'll lay a beating on you."

"You ready for this!?" I've never seen him so pumped, I'm pumped too. I rip open my envelope as well and skim through it to discover the same information.

"Hell yes!" I say as we high five. "Let's see what group we got." I start to read the rest of the letter. "Am I reading this right?"

"What do you mean?"

"It says we got diamond one. That's the highest division. That means we're in the top 20 of our class."

"Of course you're reading it right! Never doubted us for a second, of course we're diamond one."

"That means we might have to fight on day one."

"Only if they wanna kick the season off with a bang," Clarence says, "gotta show off your best fighters first and foremost right?"

"Yeah I guess."

"Excuse you, you just got matched up with the biggest toughest guy in this school, and assigned to the best group possible, and all you can say is 'Yeah I guess'? I wanna hear some confidence. I wanna hear some excitement. Most of all, I wanna hear you tell me what we're gonna do!"

"We're gonna win!" I shout and laugh.

"Now tell me who got this!?"

"We got this man," I say with confidence. I honestly feel a lot more confident knowing that Clarence will have my back out on the battle field, I feel a fire in my belly and for the first time I am actually excited for the arena.

After Clarence and I get over our initial excitement I listen to the rest of the train. I notice a plethora of emotions. Some are relieved from being in doubles or about what group they got, and others are depressed for the same reasons. When you've gone to school with the same people for 18 years you know most of them pretty well, and you see some stand out from the rest. I know there are a few people that I hope we aren't facing in our first match.

"I wonder what Gordon and Joseph got," Clarence says.

"I don't know, I can't say I'm really hopeful either way. If they got doubles we might have to fight them eventually, but if they got singles they can't have each other's backs out there."

"I'm sure it will all work out, we have to live up to that toast after all, gotta have the whole crew together for New Year's."

Before long an orderly comes by with a cart and hands us our breakfast. We are having brown rice, chicken, and a fruit bowl with water. The orderly then hands us a piece of paper and a pencil. "Select what you would like for lunch," he says, "I'll be by to pick them up shortly." I look at the list and see that sushi is listed. *YES.* This day is already going a million times better than I expected. Not only am I in doubles with Clarence, and in the top group, but I am getting sushi for lunch? Yes please.

"Man I can't wait for this tour crap to be over," Clarence says with a mouth full of food. "We gotta get going with some training, work out some sick combo moves."

"We should have plenty of time, just gotta look good for the outside world first, then we train hard."

"I got all sorts of ideas, just have to put in the hours, which we will."

I haven't really thought about it until now, but I just realized that we are going to be on that train for six hours, and then we are going to be doing some sort of agenda for the show's benefit. This is the first day that we haven't done some sort of training. Ever. It's weird, but it's nice. It's a pleasant change of pace to be able to just sit and be lazy.

After we finish eating the orderly comes back by and collects our plates and papers. Now we just sit here, there's nothing to do really. I was hoping that I would be able to see the outside world, but there are no windows on the train. I have no idea if we are outside, underground, or even underwater for that matter.

Several hours pass, there isn't much to talk about. Clarence and I don't really know what to expect when we get there, all we know is that it's a way to show case up and coming talent for rich people who like the show. We just sit here and let our minds wander. I wonder what it will be like, I don't know if we will actually get to see the outside world, or any of its people for that matter, or if we will just be in doors by ourselves the entire time. Hopefully we are outside for at least a brief moment. It doesn't have to be long, just long enough to feel the wind for the first time, feel the warmth of the sun touch my skin, or even see the clouds if it's overcast, and if that's the case maybe I'll be lucky enough to experience the rain fall on my face, or see lightning flash across the sky. Even the minutest chance to set foot outside gets me excited, I know it will happen someday, but I really hope the first time isn't in the arena.

Eventually lunch time comes, and I get to have my sushi. I'm super pumped for it, I love sushi so much. The amount of pleasure that eating sushi brings me is borderline unhealthy. Best thing ever. Clarence has Steak, mashed potatoes, and carrots. I enjoy those as well, but they can't compare to sushi. Both of us devour our food. Once I finish I feel a little depressed. My stomach is satiated, but my desire for sushi is not. I could easily eat myself into a food coma if I had a limitless supply of the stuff. Before long the orderly comes by again and collects our food, less than an hour to go.

We soon hear the intercom come on again, along with the same voice as before, "Hello everyone, before we arrive at our destination, we just want to give you a few instructions and rules. First, upon arrival don't rush out of the train, exit in an orderly fashion and follow the orderlies' instructions. Second, do not try to do anything unsettling, such as trying to run, there are armed guards throughout the building we will be at, and any attempts at escape will not be tolerated." I wonder if anyone is actually dumb enough to try anything. "Finally, be on your best behavior, if all goes well this should be a painless experience for everyone." 'Should' be a painless experience, that's encouraging. "Thank you for your patience, good luck in your endeavors." As soon as the intercom cut out I feel the train start to slow, and as it slows my heart rate begins to rise. I have no idea what to expect once we got off the train, I just know whatever it is 'should' be painless.

"You ready for this?" Clarence asks. I would be seriously freaking out if I didn't have Clarence with me, he's my rock. I don't know how he does it, but Clarence always manages to keep a level head and stay confident, even in situations like this.

"Ready as I'll ever be."

"Good, time to show the world what the future doubles champions look like." He smiles and puts his hand up.

I grab it and say "Hell yes," with a smile. I didn't expect this when I woke up this morning, but I'm feeling confident, with Clarence on my side there's nothing I can't do. My greatest fear was that someday we would be forced to fight, it's a huge relief and morale boost knowing that will never happen.

The train soon comes to a stop, and after a brief pause the doors open. Everyone starts to stand and exit the train one by one. As we get to the doors and exit, I am slightly let down as I see that we are still indoors. It's not too big of a deal though, I kind of expected it. Once everyone is off the train an orderly up front starts to speak, "We will now go to the locker rooms where you will change into the outfits provided. Once you have changed, await further instructions." Once he is done speaking he turns and starts walking, and we all follow. I start looking around as we walk, the building we are in appears rather old, but nice. The floors are polished granite, the ceilings are at least 20 feet tall and have chandeliers hanging from them to light the way, and along the walls are fancy brown cylindrical pillars. It's a nice change from the dull white hallways of the academy.

After a short while we walk through a set of wooden doors into a locker room, I see hundreds of lockers without doors on them, more like tall cubbies. Every cubby has a name taped to the top of it, Clarence and I take a few minutes but eventually we find ours right next to each other. Inside the cubbies is what appears to be a… black pair of spandex underwear? *What?*

"Where's the rest of it?" Clarence says as he holds his up between his thumb and index finger.

"Maybe the rich guys are perverts?" I say.

"I don't think this is gonna fit."

"I don't think it's meant to. Not like we have much of a choice." We proceed to change.

"Yep I'm uncomfortable."

"Oh that's weird, because I feel amazingly comfortable with everything but my thing exposed to the world." Obvious sarcasm, I am beyond uncomfortable and want nothing more than to just put some clothes on. The strange black spandex covers nothing but our private areas and leaves almost nothing to the imagination. If it wasn't for me being surrounded by all of my peers I would be trying to cover myself up. However, since that's the case, I have no choice but to try and act cool and let it bother me, at least on the surface.

"Well when you put it that way I guess this isn't so bad," Clarence says jokingly, "in fact I feel rather free like this, might even be better if we did away with the spandex all together." Confident as always.

"Yeah, not sure they would be cool with that, feel free to try though."

"Maybe next time. For now I'm gonna see if I can give any of those rich people a heart attack."

"Attention," I hear a voice call from the entrance, "if I could have everyone's attention please," it's an orderly. "We will soon begin, if everyone could follow me, but first I have instructions. We will be going back stage, once we are there you will remain silent until your name is called, upon being called walk out on stage and pause in the middle until you hear the next name called. Singles will be called first, and doubles partners will go out in pairs after all the singles have gone. Be sure to smile and wave, and anything else you feel necessary. The goal of tonight is to attract votes to decide whom you'll be facing in the arena as well as bets for you once you enter the arena. Should you receive bets in your favor, five percent of all bets placed on you will be deposited into an account in your name. Should you eventually win your freedom, that money will then become yours in addition to any winnings you may earn. Profanity will not be tolerated, and any such activity shall be disciplined accordingly. Now if you'll follow me we'll be on our way." The orderly turns and starts to walk away, and everyone follows close behind.

I had heard that this was what the preseason tour was for, but I wasn't sure until now. They don't talk about it on TV, and no one really had anyone to ask, instructors and orderlies don't tell you anything even if you do ask. Rumor has it that the richest of the rich are here for a private screening of us, and they are the ones who ultimately vote on the matchups for the first week. They are supposedly also allowed to place bets on each fight, as well as an overall victor for the season. I figure it must be like horse racing, but with us in place of horses to bet on. "Damn this is exciting," Clarence says.

"What is?"

"We get to go out in front of a bunch of rich folks and make some mad money based on how studly we look," he says with a grin.

"Well in that case you and I are about to cash in." I'm trying to act confident because I know that's what Clarence wants, but the thought of parading around in skimpy underwear in front of strangers is giving me a minor heart attack.

"That's what I'm sayin'!"

After a few minutes of walking we come to another wooden door, and the orderly says, "Singles go on in, and remember no talking, doubles you will be notified when it is almost your turn. Until then remain out here and talk amongst yourselves, but keep it quiet." He turns and walks through the door and about a third of the group goes with him. There are still a few orderlies in the hallway with us to make sure we don't do anything stupid.

"How long do you think it will be?" I ask Clarence.

"Oh well last time I was here," he says, "oh wait, I've never done this before, so yeah."

"I'm thinking it'll be at least 30 minutes, maybe longer, do you see Gordon or Joseph?" We both look around for a minute. I can't see them. Part of me is sad that I don't see them, but the other part of me is happy because that hopefully means that they are singles and therefore we will never have to fight them.

"Nope, maybe they got singles, I'm sure we'll see them later."

Everyone is keeping to themselves while we sit out here, with a few exceptions. Some close friends talk to each other, and most partners have light conversation. Overall it's pretty quiet. No one really wants to talk to the competition I guess, which makes sense. Why try to get to know someone when you might have to fight them in a month? Or maybe no one wants to talk to other guys in skimpy underwear while wearing skimpy underwear. "Hey man," Clarence says with a whisper, "I have an idea."

"What?" I ask as quietly as I can. I don't know that the whispering is necessary, but if he thinks he has some fancy super-secret awesome plan, I'll play along. Maybe his plan involves more clothes.

"When we get in there, we should do some pushups and sit-ups and stuff, that way we get a good pump for when we go on stage. Look good in front of everyone, you know?"

"Sounds good to me." I'm not going to say anything, but if we start randomly doing push-ups in the middle of the room once we get in there, people will likely notice. I'm not about to kill his joy though. It's a good idea, it just won't be a very well kept secret. This is adding to my anxiety though because now we will not only be dressed the way we are, but we will be doing pushups and draw attention to ourselves so everyone can see just how ridiculous we look. I know everyone else probably feels the same, but that's besides the point.

We stand in the hallway for quite some time before anything happens. Finally, after about an hour, the door opens and an orderly waves us in. As we pass through the door there is a second orderly pointing where we need to go with one hand, and his other hand with a finger to his lips signifying that we need to be quiet. It's dark, with just barely enough light to see. As we go deeper into the room I can see a large black curtain with light on the edge of it and an orderly standing by it. Every 15 seconds or so a name gets called out over a speaker and someone walks into the light. Obviously that is where we are supposed to enter from. With every name called as they walk on stage there is an announcer stating facts about them such as "skilled in martial arts" or "top of his class in archery," things of that nature. The announcer is basically trying to hype people up with whatever facts he has on us. As soon as there is only a few people left from the singles Clarence starts doing push-ups, so I do the same. Push-ups and sit-ups, and after I feel a good enough pump I start doing slow concentration curls with just my arms to get my biceps pumped up. Clarence gives me a thumbs up and does the same. I'm confident that to everyone around us we look like idiots, oh well, no turning back now.

As soon as they finish the singles, the announcer states that it is time for doubles to go. The first names called are Ricardo and Andrew, I'm surprised as I see the two people walking towards the curtain. I had never talked to them before but I recognize them from our cardio class. It feels messed up, but I'm happy that I don't know them on a personal level. I honestly wish that I didn't know any of the people standing with us personally, the less I know the easier the fights will be on my conscience.

After about 15 seconds or so we hear the next names "And our second duo, a dangerous diamond level force to be reckoned with, ROYCE AAAAANNND CLARENCE!" I'm surprised that we are second, but at the same time I'm glad because I want to get it over with sooner than later. Clarence pats me on the shoulder and jumps a few times to get psyched on the way to the curtain. I follow close behind and we walk out side by side, me on the left and him on the right.

The lights are hot, and so bright they are almost blinding. I still manage smile and stand tall with my chest, back and abs flexed to look good. Clarence has a huge smile on and flexes his right arm. "The deadly duo of Clarence and Royce are both in the top one percent of their class in hand to hand combat, cardio, and their respective weapons training. Clarence is all offense and a skilled swordsman, with preference on dual wielding scimitars. Royce is a master at defense, with his weapon of choice being the spear with a shield when available. This dynamic doubles team is sure to put on a great show and go far!" We pause at center stage and do multiple poses with our muscles flexed at the crowd, or at least what I am assuming is a crowd. The lights are so bright that I can't see anything past the stage. I'm sure if there is a crowd however, that they can see literally everything there is to see thanks to the lights. "Next up, we have the terrifying pairing of DAMIAN AAANNDD NICHOLAS!" The announcer yells, and with that we walk off stage. I feel pretty good about what we did, kind of.

Once off stage we are directed through a door back into another hallway where only Ricardo and Andrew are waiting. It feels awkward, so we avoid them and stand near opposite them. I assume that since they are just standing there that we have to wait for the rest of everyone else to go on. "You hear that!?" Clarence asked excitedly under his breath.

"Hear what?" I asked quietly.

"Top one percent! I told you we we're studs."

"I knew we were good, I just didn't know we were THAT good. Who knew they tracked stuff like that?"

"Makes sense when you are trying to get a bunch of rich people to throw money down on your matches. I mean if I wasn't feeling good about our chances when I found out we were partners, I sure am now! We got this man, diamond one for a reason!" Clarence's confidence makes me feel pretty good, I honestly had no idea that we were in the top of our class, I just knew that we were good. Part of me thought we might be low end diamond one, barely making the cut, but this boosts my confidence.

We stand in the hallway for quite some time. The rest of the group funnels in at a pretty steady rate. Finally, after an eternity, an orderly speaks up, "Attention please, that concludes our initial presentation, now we will move onto the meet and greet. If you could all follow me, we will be going into an open room where the audience will be able to get an up close look at you. You have each been assigned a number, which is the same as your seat on the train, find your number on the floor and stand on it. You are not permitted to speak unless spoken to. If you are asked a question, answer it to the best of your ability. They will be allowed to touch you, but you are under no circumstances allowed to touch them. Let's be on our way." With that he turns and starts off down the hall.

The room he spoke of is more of an open arena with hundreds of conic lights that illuminate small areas above each number, so it's as if each person is in the spotlight. Clarence and I wander for a couple minutes before finally finding numbers 121 and 122 under the same light. "Keep your chin up and be sure to look pretty," Clarence whispers with a smile."

"So act normal, got it."

We stand on our numbers waiting for about ten minutes with our respective hands interlaced over our crotches. Even though we are used to the lack of clothing, it doesn't mean we feel comfortable, and I don't really know what else to do with my hands. Finally doors on the opposite end from where we walked in open and people in tuxedos and fancy dresses flood in. It's strange seeing people dressed so formal, I have only ever seen pictures of clothing like that, I don't really get the appeal besides the fact that the women's dresses are shiny. I'm also surprised to see women mixed into the group, since we have never been up close to women, it's not that great though because most of these women appear to be significantly older than us. There are almost as many of them as us. It feels slightly uncomfortable, they are looking over us one by one passing by, but they aren't really looking at all of us. It's as if each of them has specific people they are looking for. The first one to walk up to us is an overweight short man in a tux that appears to be in his sixties. He looks Clarence over from head to toe, and now me. He pokes my arm and chest a few times. I feel super uncomfortable, and slightly violated, but I manage to keep a straight face with my eyes forward. "Hmph" is all he says as he walks away. Was that 'hmph' a good hmph or a bad hmph? I have no idea if we are even doing this right, but I don't want to really do anything to draw attention since it might get us in trouble, plus I don't really want that many people touching me, especially old guys.

For the next hour we get what I feel like is a lot of attention compared to the people around us. Dozens of the viewers walk up and look us over. Some touch or poke us, some ask us questions like "Are you a winner?" to which we always answer yes, and others ask us to do things like flex for them. Many of the women give us perverse smiles, which is creepy an unsettling, but flattering on some level I guess. There are a few weird ones in the mix too, one guy asks us how many pushups we can do, we just say a lot, and then he asks us to show him. We do push-ups for about two minutes before he tells us to stop. Another woman walks up and places each of our hands at our sides, and then she grabbed our crotches. It's perhaps the most uncomfortable moment of my life, needless to say I can't keep a straight face. One rather odd looking man lifts our arms and smells our armpits. I guess everyone has their own way of deciding if someone is worth betting on. This entire spectacle makes me feel like less of a human and more of a doll. It's as if we are just here for their amusement, which I guess is the point of the arena when I think about it, but still I never want to do this again. Why can't these creeps just look at our stats from the academy and place bets off of those?

Finally after what feels like hours of being looked over, questioned, smelt, and groped, an orderly at the entrance they came from speaks up, "Ladies and gentlemen, if you'll follow me the female presentation will begin shortly." Some intermittent chatter begins amongst them as they all make their way out. I wasn't aware the girls were here too, I can't help but wonder if Dime is here. I hope that she is, maybe I will have a chance to see her face to face. I doubt it, but a guy can dream. Even if it's only for a moment.

Once all the spectators have left the room an orderly at the entrance we came from says, "Thank you for your cooperation, now if you'll follow me I'll take you back to the locker room where you can change back into your uniforms. You will then be escorted back to the train, at which time you will return to the same seat you had on the ride in. Once everyone has boarded we will wait approximately four hours for the females to finish up and board. Once they have boarded we will depart for our next location, dinner will be served shortly after departure. Again, thank you for your cooperation."

Everyone follows the orderly as he starts walking down the hall. "I guess that's why they call it a tour," I said to Clarence.

"Wonder how many stops we have to make." Clarence said.

"I'm sure they will tell us at some point, and it can't be that many, we have to train at some point or we'll get soft." I'm trying to sound like it doesn't bother me, but I was honestly crushed and angry at the same time when the orderly said we have more stops. I don't want to have to sit through more groping, one day is enough for me. I don't know if I will be able to handle this if it goes on for too much longer.

We soon get to the locker room and change back into actual clothing. I've never been so happy to put my uniform on. Once everyone is changed we are led back to the train and sit down. Once we are all in and situated, the doors to the train close. Upon the doors closing the intercom comes on and a voice says, "Your first day on the preseason tour is now complete. I'm sure you have figured out by now it is called a tour because there will be multiple stops. We will now take a moment and explain what exactly is in store for you. The tour will take five days total to complete, with four more stops planned. Next we will be stopping in Minneapolis, Minnesota, then we will head south to Dallas, Texas, after that we head to the west coast and make a stop in Los Angeles, California, and finally we end our tour in Seattle, Washington. After your final show in Seattle there will be a dance held with the females participating in the tour, at which time you will be allowed to intermingle and get to know one another. However, this dance is only for those of you who keep in line for the duration of the tour. Any who step out of line will be dealt with accordingly, and will no longer be allowed admittance to the dance. Upon completion of the dance, you will be taken to your new facility in Nevada where you will train for the remaining three weeks before the new season of The Arena begins. Thank you for your time." Then the intercom cut out.

Did I just hear that correctly? Dance? A dance with girls? This is likely some sort of ploy to not only get us to stay in line, but to get us to meet a girl and be fired up and ready to fight come time to enter the arena with hopes of seeing her again, but I don't care. If there is a dance with girls, that means Dime will hopefully be there, and if Dime is going to be there, I might finally be able to talk to her, maybe even touch her. *Oh man.* There is no way I'm going to mess this up.

The train is instantly flooded with conversation. "Dude," Clarence says.

"Yeah," I respond, "I know."

"Girls, finally!"

"I'm just hoping to find one in particular."

"Yeah I bet you are, I'm sure we'll find her man."

"Just four more days."

"That's nothing, it'll fly by."

Time passes and finally the train starts moving, apparently the girls are done and on board. The next few days are all pretty

59

similar, a lot of time spent in the train, slightly less spent in hallways, and a small amount spent on stages and inside indoor arenas. Upon arriving at each location we are allowed to use the showers in the locker rooms and brush our teeth as well. Clarence and I are popular at every location, at least I feel like we are. If these people really are looking us over in order to decide who to bet on, we are likely getting a lot of bets placed on us. It feels messed up but flattering on some level that people are betting we will kill rather than be killed. It kind of makes me wonder what is so special about us. Is it our stats? Our physical appearance? Whatever it is, I know neither of us has any intention of losing.

There are a lot of people that look us over, and a handful of weirdoes at each stop too. In Minneapolis a man asks us to do a battle cry as loud as we can. This may be the first time I've ever done a battle cry, I just yell as loud and deep as I can. In Dallas a man pulls out a stethoscope and listens to our hearts and lungs. In LA a woman asks us to do a handstand and then proceeds to push us to test our stability. Neither of us falls, which I'm pretty sure she finds impressive based on the smile across her face. The worst is in Seattle, a woman asks us to get on all fours and then sits on us one at a time and slaps our butts a few times, if I didn't feel violated before I sure do now. The entire time all of this is going on I just keep telling myself this is all worth it if I get to see Dime. I know the dance is just part of their plan to get us to fall in line, I just don't care.

III

Once we finish the Seattle show, we return to the locker rooms as usual, but when we get there our uniforms are gone. In their place are tuxedos and hair styling products, along with our usual soap and shampoo. We are told we have an hour before the dance, so everyone takes their time and showers, puts their tuxes on, and does their hair (if they have any). I didn't notice at first, but there are several different colors of tuxes. The jackets and pants are all black, but otherwise for the first time ever we aren't all dressed identically. There are dozens of different colors for shirts, vests, and ties or bow ties. The only ones with the same tuxes are doubles partners. Clarence and I have black shirts with royal blue vests and ties. We look like studs, at least I think we do.

"Damn," Clarence says, "where has this handsome man been hiding my whole life?" He's looking at himself in the mirror.

"Probably in the closet," I say.

"Haha very funny, seriously though, we look great. Tell you what, if Dime is there tonight there's no way she's gonna be able to keep her hands off of you."

"You think?"

"Um, have you looked at yourself? I mean wow, I would go there in a heartbeat if I was into that kind of thing."

"Well thanks I guess."

Once everyone is dressed we are escorted to the ballroom in which the dance is being held. There are balloons all over the floor with circular tables around the perimeter with white table cloths on top and a single rose in a vase in the center of each table. In the center of the room is a huge dance floor, lit only by the light refracted from a disco ball. There is soft music in the background. It feels refreshing to hear something other than classical music, which is all that is allowed at the academy. We are instructed to wait here for the girls, which will still be about four hours. In the meantime there is a refreshments table with snacks and water. I was hoping for something I hadn't tried before, but their definition of "snacks" is fruit, vegetables, and steak kabobs. No unfamiliar foods for us I guess. Someday I look forward to trying candy and junk food, I read in Learn Smart that junk food is so good that some people literally eat until they are so fat they can't even walk. I don't want to get that bad, but if it's that good I definitely want to try some.

Clarence and I grab a paper plate and put some food on it, then we proceed to find an empty table to sit at. We start eating and after a few minutes we are greeted by a familiar voice, "Wow they'll let anyone in here," Gordon says as he walks over with Joseph. I'm beyond happy to see them, we haven't seen them since the start of the tour.

"How you been guys?" Clarence asks as he sees them.

"Can't complain," Joseph responds.

"Yeah we were essentially the most popular guys at each location," Gordon says pompously, "so I guess you can say we're pretty good."

"I believe you are confusing yourselves for us," I say.

"So did you guys get singles or doubles?" Joseph asks.

"Doubles," Clarence responds, "and you?"

"We got singles," Gordon says, "something about it not being fair having us on a team because we would win all the matches so easily, or something like that."

"Oh, is that what they told you?" I ask.

"They didn't have to," Gordon says, "it's the only possible explanation."

"That's cool that you guys got doubles," Joseph says, "it must be nice knowing that you'll have each other's backs." It impresses me how opposite Gordon and Joseph are sometimes, Joseph shows genuine interest and cares, where Gordon talks down and brags about how awesome they are. They are polar opposites at times, and yet they are inseparable.

"Yeah I have to admit it was a relief when we found out," I tell him.

"Well it's a blessing for you really," Gordon states, "I mean you would be dead if you didn't have Clarence to carry you out there."

"Yeah okay," I scoff, "I'm sure that's how it's going to go."

"Me too," Gordon says, "that's why I said it."

"Jerk," I say.

"Love you too dear," he responds with a boyish grin. He may be a complete jerk on the surface, but he cares underneath. He will just never admit it.

I remember one time we were all sitting in the cafeteria at lunch joking around and we overheard two guys at the table behind us making fun of us. Before Joseph, Clarence, or I could even react Gordon started laughing hysterically and shouted "THAT'S SO FUNNY! I MEAN IT'S JUST SO FUNNY ISN'T IT!?" He then grabbed his tray and stood up while still laughing as he turned and put two dents in the metal tray as he hit each of them over the head.

"WHAT'S WRONG BOYS? WHY AREN'T YOU LAUGHING!? ISN'T IT FUNNY?" Gordon took a beating and a trip to the box from the orderlies, the guys making fun of us took a trip to the infirmary where I'm guessing they were diagnosed with concussions since he knocked both of them out cold.

We fill the rest of the time waiting for the girls by talking about our experiences over the past few days. We exchange stories of weirdest spectator, which Clarence and I win many times over, as well as what was said about us on stage and such. We also talk about what divisions we are in. "I mean, not to brag," Clarence says, "but my boy here and I are diamond one. We're kind of a big deal."

"Wow that's great guys!" Joseph says with his usual squinty smile, "I knew you could do it. Good job, good for you."

"This stupid system is rigged," Gordon states, "I've been performing terribly ever since I turned 17 and I still got diamond one. It's stupid." Gordon would be the guy that is upset he is in the top division.

"You didn't honestly think that sand bagging the final year would wipe out all of your previous reports and statistics did you?" I ask.

"No, but I thought it would at least be enough to drop me a few divisions. Stupid, just stupid how it works."

"Maybe they made a mistake," Clarence says with a slight laugh, "I mean if they knew how stupid your plan was they probably would have realized you should be in one of the lower divisions anyways." We all laugh aside from Gordon, who furrow's his brow.

"Well why don't you go and tell whoever is in charge this little tidbit of information and get me moved down then?"

"Sorry man no can do," Clarence responds, "besides you'll be fine. Just make sure your opponent knows you're part of my group and I'm sure they will be so scared they won't be able to keep their composure. Easy win."

64

"OH WELL WHY DIDN'T I THINK OF THAT?" Gordon shouts as he throws his hands up in the air, "THANK THE POWERS THAT BE FOR GRACING ME WITH SUCH AN INTIMIDATING FRIEND." I feel like this is what Gordon likes to do anytime he isn't getting his way, make a huge spectacle of himself. I mean it's either that or he shuts down, there is no in between.

"Anyways…" I say, "What did you wind up getting Joseph?"

"Nothing too special," Joseph responds, "Just gold three. It's no diamond one, but it's not too bad."

"Not too bad man," Clarence says, "I mean hey at least you aren't bronze or silver, I'd say that anything gold or better is respectable. Pretty sure gold is still in the top half of the class. Not too shabby man"

"Yeah Joseph, that's pretty great still when you think about it," I say reassuringly.

"Yeah," he replies, "I guess it's still pretty good, it's just unfortunate we couldn't all be diamond one is all. I'll just have to win a lot to catch up with you guys!"

"Sounds like a good plan to me," I say with a smile.

"Yeah once you thin out the competition a bit they will have to move you up for sure," Clarence adds.

"If you want diamond one so badly you could just go ask them to swap us," Gordon says, "I'd gladly swap places with you."

"Gordon man up and stop being such a pessimist," Clarence says.

"I'd rather not and say I did," Gordon responds.

"How about we stop the bickering and enjoy the night?" I suggest, "I mean this is supposed to be the last hurrah before we go into the arena, so let's enjoy ourselves guys."

"Stop it Royce," Gordon says, "Joseph is supposed to be the excessively optimistic and happy one, not you."

"I don't mind sharing the title from time to time," Joseph says.

"I'll allow it," Gordon states, "but just this once."

"Why thank you your highness for allowing me to be a positive person," I say.

"You're welcome," he responds. "Side note, Royce are you planning on meeting Dime tonight with that huge white glob on your forearm?"

"What?" I ask as I look down. My heart stops for a second as I see a sizable white spot on my forearm just above my cufflink. I can't meet Dime looking like this! "I'll be right back." I say as I excuse myself from the group and make my way to the restroom.

"Don't take too long or you'll miss out!" Gordon shouts as I leave.

Once in the restroom I grab a hand towel and try to just wipe it off, but that just smears it into my jacket. Eventually I decide to just put my entire forearm under running water and scrub like my life depends on it. I can't believe I Was stupid enough to get food on my suit. All I can think about is what Dime is going to think if she sees me with a huge stain on my suit and how embarrassing that would be. That would be a great way to make a memorable first impression though, "Hi I'm Royce and clearly I don't know how to keep food in my mouth." Finally I manage to get the spot out, after what seems like an eternity, however I am now faced with the dilemma that is a soaking wet forearm. I try to dab it with dry towels, but they have little to no effect. I see an air dryer for hands on the wall so I hurry over to it and turn it on. I'm sure I look awfully impressive to the guys that are slowly trickling in and out of the bathroom, seeing me just standing here with my wet forearm under an air dryer. This is taking far too long, at this rate the dance will be over before I'm even able to get back out there. That would be my luck, my first opportunity to meet Dime face to face and I spend the entire time in the bathroom. Gordon would never let me live it down. I wish there was a power dry button on this thing, even if it burned me I'd give it a go just to be able to get back out there. Finally it dries, there is a very slight discoloration, but at least it's not a huge white blob for everyone to see. Time to head back out onto the floor.

I exit the bathroom and everything has changed since I left. It's no longer just a bunch of guys standing around talking to each other, now the entire floor is packed with girls and guys intermingling, talking, and dancing. It's so packed that I can't see anyone that I recognize. I start to panic slightly, what if I can't find my way back to my group? What if my group has all split up and found girls of their own? Then it dawns on me, Dime is walking around somewhere in this crowd. What if she is talking to another guy? What if I can't find her? There are so many possibilities that I don't know what to do, so I just start making my way through the middle of the crowd.

After a few minutes I feel an all too familiar sensation, and I know that Dime is nearby. I start to look around me, but I can't see anything in a crowd that is so tightly packed together. I wander aimlessly, trying to follow the sensation to her, but unfortunately it doesn't act as a compass so much as a really poor radar. Maybe I won't find her after all. Right as I start to doubt myself I feel a tap on the back of my right shoulder. I turn and everything in the room comes to a crawl, and time seemingly stops. There she is, right before my very eyes, only a breath away from me. Here I am looking for her and it's her that finds me. She's so beautiful, wearing a strapless ocean blue dress that matches her deep blue eyes. Her hair is curled and has a blue flower in it, and she has blue shoes to match. Breathtaking, to say the least. I smile at her, and she has a smile to match. We just stand there for a moment, not doing anything. I finally start to raise my right arm 90 degrees and stretch my hand out flat and perpendicular to the ground. She does the same and our hands touch for the first time. My eyes close for a moment and I take a deep breath. I'm really touching her. After 12 years of never being able to make contact, my skin is now one with hers for the first time.

My eyes open, but my vision is slightly blurred. I realize there are tears welling up in my eyes. This moment has been a long time coming, and I can't help but tear up a bit because of it. I wipe my eyes with my sleeve and look over to see her doing the same. We both laugh slightly. The pitch of her laughter is cute and adorable, so much higher than I've ever heard before. Once we finish laughing she opens her mouth as though she's about to speak.

"HI I'M GORDON!" he would. How did he even find us? His timing is impeccable, why is this happening?

"NOT NOW!" I say very sternly under my breath to him.

"WELL SOOOOORRRRRYYY! My bad for trying to introduce myself, your best friend and role model, to your girlfriend. I guess we'll just have to do this later then!" I hate him. Gordon walks off and now I'm just standing here awkwardly in front of Dime not knowing what to say or do.

"Sorry about that. Please disregard and start fresh?" I say.

"Okay, Hi," she says with a smile, oh man her voice is so smooth and warm, she only said one word but the sound flowed like a river and washed over me, if I was crippled before, I am paralyzed now, lost in the echo of her voice resonating in my mind.

"Hi," I just realized that I'm about to talk to Dime for the first time, and I have no idea what I'm going to say.

"Hi," she lets out a short laugh. It's hard to describe all of the emotions going through me, I'm excited to meet her, but I'm scared I'll do something dumb. I'm comfortable around her because I feel like I already know her, but I feel awkward actually being this close to her with nothing to keep us apart. Even my heart feels like it wants to beat fast and slow at the same time. I'm all conflicted inside.

68

I look around and see that a lot of the people around us have started to dance, well they are doing what appears to be dancing. Really its just a lot of people spinning in circles and stepping on their partner's feet. "Should we, uh, partake?"

"Are you asking me to dance?" She raises and eyebrow and smiles from the corner of her mouth.

"I mean, only if you want to?"

"I think I'd like that." We are already standing in the middle of the dance floor so I simply step closer to her. She puts her hands on my shoulders, and I put my hands on her hips. We start to slowly move on circles. I'm not sure if she's ever danced before, but the guys never learn to. I've read about it in my learn smarts, so I'm simply imitating what I think is right. I could be completely wrong. "Ow!" She says, "Watch your feet!"

"Sorry!" I can't believe I'm dumb enough to step on her feet like every other guy. She steps on mine a few moments later, but I don't say anything. At least I'm not the only one doing it. "I've been waiting for this for eleven years."

"Me too. It's weird to think about how we've never actually met, but I feel like I already know you, and I don't even know your name."

"Royce."

She smiles, "Kayleah."

"Nice to finally meet you, Kayleah."

"Nice to formally meet you, Royce."

"So there's something I've wanted to say for a few years now, but I haven't because it just wouldn't feel right if it weren't in person like this."

"What's that?"

"I'm sorry about getting you sent to the box, it was never my intention, and it killed me knowing that it was my fault."

"Don't feel bad, I wouldn't have put my hand on the glass if I didn't want to. I knew we were breaking the rules." I can't help but smile as she says this. I don't know what I expected her to say, but it would have killed me if she was upset about it.

"I hope you know I never stopped thinking about you for those two years, I found myself looking for you every day, even if I knew you wouldn't be there."

"I caught myself doing the same more often than not. It was hard not seeing you every day. I lit up when I finally saw you again. It was like someone put the missing piece back in my chest and a weight had been lifted off of me. Seeing you is one of the few things I look forward to most days." It's like she was made for me, everything she's saying is exactly how I feel.

"You're part of what's kept me going, knowing that if I do well I'd get to meet you eventually, and knowing now that if I continue to do well I'll see you again. I don't know what this feeling is, but I know I want to explore it. I want to see where this leads us. I want to know what the future holds for us, and I want it to be good."

"I guess that means we'll just have to win our matches so we can see each other again then doesn't it?"

"I mean that's basically the plan right now."

"Have you ever thought about what you'll do if you make it out?"

"I've never really give it much thought. I'm not really sure, but I know I want to experience nature. I want to go outside and just feel the sun touch my skin. I want to walk barefoot through the grass, or feel mud between my toes. I want to feel the wind and smell the flowers. I feel caged, and I just want to be free. So I guess that's what I'll do, what about you?"

"I just know that I'll be getting as far away from the arena as possible, maybe I'll go experience nature with you."

"I'd like that. We can work out the details when we get to that point, though. Long road ahead and all."

"Yeah, but you've got to have goals to keep you going, if you have nothing to look forward to how are you supposed to stay motivated?"

"I've never really thought about it like that. I guess I've always just worked hard so I can stay alive and see my friends and you again after every fight."

"I think our goals are what keep us alive, and if you lose track of them you come up short in the end."

"Well now that I have a goal I'll just have to stay focused won't I?"

"You better. If you lose I'll kick your butt!" She scrunches her face.

"Oh is that so? I'm not sure how that's possible, but I'm not going to lose so it shouldn't be a problem."

"Do you remember the first time we locked eyes?"

"How could I forget? We were six, you had just won a sparring match and smiled as you looked up and saw me."

"I never would have thought in that moment, that the boy staring awkwardly at me from across the glass would grow to be important to me like you have. It's crazy. First it was an awkward gaze, then an awkward smile and wave, and eventually even awkwardly putting your hand on the glass for me. Looking back at it, where we started and where we are now, it's sort of hard to believe."

"So I'm awkward huh?"

"You are!" She laughs and my face droops a bit, "It's not a bad thing though, it's actually the opposite. It's the awkward things you do that show how genuine you are. It makes you real to me. Lots of the boys are constantly goofing off or trying to look tough to get a rise out of the girls. You can't fake awkward, it makes you unique and separates you from everyone else. How many boys would smile and wave at a girl the day after she accidentally smiles at them?"

"Just one I guess," I shrug my shoulders.

"Exactly! And that's what makes you so great."

"Never thought someone would call me awkward as a compliment, but I guess that works. Thanks."

"No, thank you." She wraps her hands around my neck and pulls herself in closer.

It's hard to believe how close we are to each other right now. Our bodies fit so perfectly together, it's as if we are meant to be like this. She's so much shorter than I am, but it's as if we were built for each other. Her firm body curves in all the right places to fit perfectly against mine. There are no gaps between us. I lower my head and rest my cheek against the top of her head. As I take a deep breath I breathe in her scent for the first time. It encapsulates me. On the surface I smell the fresh scent of shampoo that the orderlies provide us with, but that isn't what is drawing me in. Underneath the shampoo I can smell HER smell. It's intoxicating, yet clarifying, stimulating, yet relaxing, foreign, yet familiar. I take a deep breath and allow her essence to enter my lungs and fill my chest with desire. My eyes close and my jaw quivers slightly as I exhale and feel her flowing through me. As of this moment, I never want to be apart from her again.

"Alright let's wrap things up everyone, we have a schedule to keep," I hear a voice say from across the room. An orderly is standing at the entrance. "Ladies if you'll follow me I'll escort you to the locker room so you can change before we depart. Gentlemen someone will be by to escort you shortly. Let's get a move on people." I could feel my heart sink.

"So I guess this is goodbye," I sigh with dismay.

"This isn't goodbye," she shrugs, "it's simply until next time."

"Stealing my lines."

"It's kept us going this long hasn't it?"

"Well then, until next time." At that moment we lock eyes again, people are already starting to leave, but we haven't moved an inch. I'm not sure how this is possible, but it feels as though my heart is beating faster as time slows down. She closes her eyes and leans in, a whisper away from my face. I don't know why I am closing my eyes, but it feels right, like you are supposed to close them. Our lips touch, and I go up in flames. I feel all powerful, yet vulnerable at the same time. Her lips are soft and moist, her gentle hands grasp tighter around my neck. I try to pull her closer to me, but she is already pressed tightly against my body. I take a deep breath through my nostrils, drawing in her smell one last time, giving me goose bumps and adding to the impact of this moment. Time stopped, but only for a moment, and once that moment passes, and our lips part, I feel weak. If our bodies weren't pressed so tightly against one another, I would probably fall over. The perfect moment has passed, and I already want it back. We both smile as she starts to leave. She holds onto my hand as long as possible as she slowly starts to walk away until just our fingers are touching, and now we are apart again.

"Until next time, Royce," she says smiling as she walks off.

"Until next time, Kayleah" The words are so soft they are nearly a whisper as they leave my lips. She soon walks through the door, and then she's gone.

"MY MAN!" Clarence shouts as he walks up and grabs my shoulders, "My boy's got game! How was it?"

"How was what?"

"How was what? Um, well let me see. How about the kiss?! Or just the entire dance for that matter."

"Amazing, just amazing."

"Guess we're gonna have to do this again sometime then."

"I could get on board with that idea. How was your night?"

"Well I didn't meet the love of my life, but I got to dance with a few girls and got a kiss at the end if that's what you're asking. I can't complain."

"Sounds like we both had fun then."

"You know it, you and me are the alpha dogs around here, of course we're gonna get some mad action."

"Hah, sure thing."

"Let's go gentlemen, we have a schedule to keep," the orderly at the entrance says. We start walking back to the locker room, our uniforms are back in the cubbies. We change and then are escorted back to the train.

"We will soon depart for Nevada, thank you for your continued patience," the intercom says once everyone is inside. Before long the train starts to move.

"Fun time is over now," Clarence says once the train starts moving.

"Time to get serious."

"We have three weeks until we have to tear up the arena, that means we have three weeks to become the biggest toughest guys this country has ever seen."

"Better rest up then, tomorrow is going to be a big day."

"We got this, nothing to it but to do it." He holds his fist out and we fist bump. This really is the time to get serious, the training over the next three weeks is all we have to prepare us for the arena, and after tonight there is no way I'm going to lose out in the first round and miss the chance to see Kayleah again. There's a lot riding on our success, and I have absolutely no intention of failing.

IV

"We will soon be arriving at our destination," the voice over the intercom states, "upon arrival please exit the train and await further instructions from arena staff." The intercom cuts out. This is it, we are finally at our final training destination. The last stop on the way to the arena. I'm ready.

The new training center is located on the outskirts of Las Vegas, which is where the show takes place. What better place to have a show where people fight to the death than Sin City? Countless tourists to go to the show, as well as an abundance of people with gambling problems.

When the train comes to a stop Clarence and I look at each other and nod, there's nothing to say, we know it's time to get down to business once we receive our instructions. As we exit the train an orderly is waiting at the head of the crowd to tell us where to go, he has a scanner on each side of him, just like when we left the academy. "Make two lines, single file," he shouts over the crowd, "doubles will be on the left, singles on the right. Scan in to receive room assignments, doubles will be down the hall to the left, and singles down the hall to the right. Singles will have their own room to avoid conflict between combatants, doubles partners will bunk up together just as you did at the academy. The rules here are the same as the academy, be on your best behavior or you will be dealt with accordingly. Any attempt at sabotaging another combatant will not be taken lightly and will result in a 48 hour stay in the box." 48 hours is unheard of for the box, but I guess that's to ensure that no one starts fights outside of the arena. The atmosphere is going to be tense amongst combatants from here on out. Everyone is a potential threat. "You will have three weeks to prepare before the first fights of the season begin. From here on out you will make your own schedules, the cafeteria will be open all day, and you will be allowed to scan in for three meals each day. Wake-up call will come at 6am, and lights out will be at 10pm, that gives you 16 hours to do with as you please. A map of the compound is provided in each room, as well as your uniforms for the next three weeks. It is now 10am, which gives you 12 hours before curfew, we suggest you get your affairs in order and begin preparations as soon as possible. That concludes your briefing." This is a lot to take in, but it sounds fairly similar to the academy, I just want to get going.

Clarence and I stand together in the left line and wait our turn. We receive our room assignment and follow the hall to the left, this compound seems to be nearly identical to the academy; the halls are all white. We get to our room and step inside to find that even it is identical to our old room. There is a map of the compound on the nightstand. On it we notice a room labeled "Combat Simulator". We agree that we need to check it out at some point.

Clarence and I decide that we should start things off with weights. We both change and start walking towards the weight room. We ate a few hours ago on the train, so we aren't that hungry, and we really need to lift since we haven't done much while out on tour. Plus we are both super pumped up and ready to get going with the arena right around the corner. These next three weeks could easily decide whether we win or lose. There are three weight rooms in the compound on three different floors, Clarence suggests that we use the third level since most people will probably flock to the first one since its closest.

When we get there I notice Clarence is right, the third floor isn't very crowded. There's still a decent amount of people here, but nothing compared to the first floor. We scan in and walk into the middle of the room to decide where to go first. "Man, I didn't know they let girls lift on this side too!" A familiar voice says, I look to see Gordon walking our way with a big grin across his face. He was obviously proud of his entrance. Joseph was with him too, as per usual.

"You lost?" Clarence asks as they shake hands and pat each other on the back.

"We figured there would be less people up here," Joseph says.

"Yeah we thought there wouldn't be as many losers, apparently we were wrong," Gordon adds.

"Why do you have to talk about yourself like that?" I ask Gordon.

"Self-motivation to do better," he states.

"So what are you guys doing today?" Clarence asks.

"Back and biceps," Joseph says.

"Nice," I say, "us too. Wanna make this a four-some?"

"That sounds dirty," Gordon says, "I like it, just no biting okay?" Leave it to Gordon to take it to the next level.

"This place is decently empty," Clarence states, "shouldn't be hard to get equipment next to each other."

"Let's get to it," Joseph says.

"TO THE SQUAT RACKS!" Gordon shouts with a fist in the air as he turns and charges over to the nearest one.

"I'm going to assume he wants to start with bent-over row," Clarence says, "because otherwise he's an idiot."

"Yeah we always start with bent-over row," Joseph says as we walk over to the squat racks.

We all warm up and then start doing our working sets. "You know I've been doing some thinking," Gordon says in between sets.

"Oh no, not again," Clarence says. We all laugh.

"For real though," Gordon says, "this is some deep stuff."

"You say that every time," I say mid set.

"Well, you see," he raises his hands as if they are going to help us understand what he's about to explain, "When Royce ultimately takes the longest to earn his freedom due to Clarence having a hard time carrying the burden that is his doubles partner, someone is going to have to take care of Kayleah until he gets out. Now I know what you're thinking, who could that be? Who is going to be so kind as to take care of Royce's lifelong crush? Well, when I inevitably win my freedom and set foot upon the outside world before any of you losers, I have decided that I shall carry that burden. I shall do you this favor Royce, so that Joseph doesn't have to. Love me, for I am kind."

I'm sure he can tell I'm less than enthused by the drop in my stature, "You seem awfully confident with that theory." I say. The grin across his face grows.

"Just thought I'd do you a solid! I mean you're probably going to take so long that your girl will inevitably get tired of waiting and choose a better man anyways."

"One problem with that story," Clarence says, "my boy here is gonna kill it! You see, we're going hard all the way!" At least Clarence has faith in me.

"I'm sure we're all going to make it at the same time," Joseph says with a smile in an attempt to lighten the mood. Leave it to Gordon to put a damper on the atmosphere.

"Hey optimism is fun and all, I'm just trying to prepare for a few alternatives that's all. You're welcome."

"Yeah, thanks, I guess," is all I can say. It's like he just enjoys pushing people's buttons at times.

We continue on with our workout and Gordon keeps trying to make light of his stupid joke, while slowly digging a deeper hole for himself. We did various back workouts, and then it was time to finish up with some biceps, so we went over to the preacher station to do some curls. "Ah yes, the preacher station. The perfect spot to do some reps for Jesus." Gordon states.

"You're ridiculous, let's just leave it at that," Clarence says.

"Let's do some negatives to finish strong," I say. I'm hoping doing something hard will shut him up.

Negatives are when you only do the downward portion of the rep, or the negative portion, and you go as slow as possible. Once you hit the bottom you have your lifting partner lift the weight back up for you and you do it again. I went first, after my eighth rep I curled the weight and then started to lower it as slowly as possible for the negative. "You're a piece of garbage, your parents never loved you, we all hate you, and you are a disgustingly hideous person whom no one can stand to look at," Gordon says. I start laughing and drop the weight.

"What was that?" I ask.

"You said we are doing negatives," Gordon says, "so I was channeling as much negative energy towards you as possible in order to help."

"Where do you come up with this stuff?" Clarence asks.

"I mean it's just simple science when you think about it," Gordon states. "In fact, it all makes perfect sense if you don't think about it. We can do positives after this if it makes you feel better."

"I forgot you guys had never lifted with Gordon before," Joseph says. "He does this literally every time, in fact I don't know that anyone could hurt my feelings with words after hearing some of the stuff he comes up with. I'm essentially immune to it now." Maybe that's why Joseph is so happy all the time, Gordon beat the sad out of him.

"What exactly are positives?" I ask.

"Same as negatives," Gordon says, "except you go up instead of down and someone pulls on the bar to make it so that it barely moves while I channel all my positive energy into you. Do a set real quick and I'll show you."

"I feel like I'm going to regret this," I say. "Eight regular reps, followed by four positives?"

"Yep!" Gordon says. I knock out my eight reps and then start my positives, going up while Gordon pulls on the bar just hard enough that I can barely lift the weight. "You're a wonderful person. Woah, those biceps are huge! Do you lift often? I can tell. Man with biceps that big I can only imagine how big your penis is, that thing must be a monster!" I drop the weight again, everyone is laughing, and I'm to the point where tears are rolling down my cheeks I'm laughing so hard.

"How do you workout with this guy?" Clarence asks Joseph.

"It was difficult at first," Joseph said, "but you get used to it. Worst case scenario I get a good ab workout from laughing too hard."

"I feel like this is why we are bigger than you guys," Clarence says. I'm still on the ground trying to catch my breath. My throat and stomach hurt from laughing too much.

"I feel like the lack of steroids is also a plausible explanation," Gordon states.

"Yeah because the academy was secretly slipping us steroids and just decided not to give you any," Clarence says.

"I'm glad we're on the same page," Gordon says. I finally manage to regain my composure and stand up.

"Nope," Clarence says.

"Never say never!" Gordon says with enthusiasm.

"I didn't say never, I said nope," Clarence responds.

"Same difference," Gordon says.

"No it isn't," Clarence states.

"Yes it is. It's exactly the same difference, I didn't say same thing."

"I can't handle this," Clarence says, he walks over to the dumbbells to do more curls.

"Good job on that one," I say. "We are probably gonna go ahead and do our own thing, you guys planning on doing weights every day first thing?"

"If you guys are then probably," Joseph says.

"Talk to you guys tomorrow then," I say as I start to walk over to join Clarence by the dumbbells.

Gordon managed to remind us just how big of a pain he can be sometimes. We each do a few sets of curls and then call it good and head back to our room, which takes longer than it should since we get turned around a few times. It's going to take a while before we manage to get used to this new facility.

When we get back to our room we hit the showers and then change into our combat uniform, aside from lunch the rest of the day is going to be intense training. We head to the cafeteria to eat, when we find it we are pleased by the sight of a relatively empty room. Most people are most likely still training or trying to get used to the layout of the new facility, so we will get to eat in peace. "That's what I'm talkin' about!" Clarence says ecstatically. "No lines baby! WOO!" This is the first time we have ever been able to just walk straight up to the scanner and get our food, it feels pretty good.

We each get served the same food; steamed chicken, rice, and vegetables with water. It's basic, but still better than super food. We are already a little behind schedule, so we eat quickly. We want to be able to spend as much time as possible exploring and training, that way future days will go by smoother. Once we finish we clear our trays and start walking towards the hallway. We decide to check out the combat simulator next.

When we get to the area marked on the map there is a set of large crimson red doors that read "Combat Simulators". We push them open to see that the hallway continues, but it's dimly lit with red lighting instead of the bright white we usually see. In this new hallway there are doors on either side of the hall every 40 feet or so. Outside of each door is a scanner and a computer screen. The first few doors' computers say "Session in progress" across the screen. I figure that means that they are occupied. We finally find one that says "Please scan intended combatants."

"Ready?" Clarence asks.

"Nothing to it but to do it, right?" I respond.

We each scan in and the screen brings up our pictures and then switches to a screen that says "Please select intended training." There are all sorts of options listed, from hand to hand combat, to weapons training, to projectiles. "Uh, projectiles?" Clarence asks.

"Let's give it a shot," I reply. Clarence selects projectiles and then the screen changes again, "Select difficulty," it lists four options: beginner, intermediate, advanced, and ultimate. "Try beginner and see how it goes?"

"Sure," Clarence says as he selects it.

"Select weapons of choice," appears on the screen next. Clarence selects dual wield scimitars and I select shield and spear. "Please enter, when ready stand in white circle to begin. We open the door and step inside. The room is roughly 40 feet wide and 100 feet long, the walls and floors are all black with the floors being matted. In the center of the room is a white illuminated circle, the rest of the room was lit by the same red lighting as the hallway. To our left we can see our weapons sitting on the wall, it looks as though they came out of the wall from the metal panels they are sitting on. They are training weapons just like back at the academy.

We grab our respective weapons. It feels good to have my hands on a spear and shield again, it has been far too long. Clarence grabs his scimitars and spins them around in his hands a few times with a big grin on his face. "Let's get this show on the road!" he says as he starts walking over to the white circle, I follow close behind. We are both jumping up and down and shaking our arms and legs out in preparation. Neither of us know what to expect, but we are both excited. With my spear in my left hand, and my shield on my right arm, I'm ready.

As soon as we enter the circle the far wall lights up with a projection, it's a timer counting down from 10. We both enter our ready stances facing the wall, I crouch behind my shield with my body at a slight angle and my spear rested against the side of my shield. Clarence does a slight lunge with one leg forward, on his toes, his body at a 45 degree angle to the wall with his back to me, arms slightly bent at his sides, and his scimitars angled so they are almost touching at their point in front of him. We are ready.

As soon as the clock strikes zero it disappears, and two projections that resemble men appear in its place. They each have what appear to be bows, which they quickly draw and fire at us. It's so surreal to see the projections of the arrows flying at us, I only have time to admire the technology for but a moment though, because I quickly have to raise my shield to block the arrow fired at me, Clarence sliced his in half with his scimitars. "Awesome," I say. The projections don't waste any time, they start running to the side and firing arrow after arrow at us, I throw my shield up and block them easy enough, Clarence just keeps chopping his out of the air. "I think we have to kill the projections," I say.

"Sounds about right." Clarence starts to run towards his respective projection, as he does I see mine turn to fire at him. I lower my shield quickly and take a step forward as I launch my spear at my projection, hitting it right in the chest and pinning it to the wall. *That's so cool.* Clarence quickly closes the gap on his projection and delivers a killing blow to its neck. This is by far the coolest thing we have ever done. "That wasn't so bad," Clarence says, "Let's take it up a notch."

"Let's do it," I say. Clarence sets his scimitars by the white circle and jogs over to the door, he steps out for a second then comes jogging back in. "What did you set it to?" I ask as he picks up his weapons.

"Ultimate," He says with a smile.

"Well then, I guess we'll find out what that means shortly."

We both step into the white circle and wait for the countdown again, once it finishes it spawns two archers again. And yet again they draw their bows and fire. We each go to block them and then I look over at the archers and they are already firing again. *Uh oh.* The archers are running around and firing arrows from all directions, it's difficult to keep up with. Clarence is even on the defensive and slowly backing up to give himself more time to block each arrow. "Screw this!" I yell as I lower my shield and throw my spear at an archer, it's on target to hit, and then the archer dives to avoid it. I missed completely. I suddenly feel a pain in my shoulder and fall to the ground. When I dropped my shield to throw my spear the other archer reacted and fired at my exposed shoulder. Apparently the arrows actually hurt too, because when it hits me I feel a searing pain in my shoulder. Once I'm hit the archers disappeared.

"Smooth," Clarence says as he walks over. "You ok?"

"Yeah," I say as I rub my shoulder," those things sure do hurt though."

"Try not to get hit then."

"Oh well gee, I guess I never thought of that, thanks for the advice mister 'let's try ultimate and see what happens."

"I didn't think it was that bad," he says.

"You were slowly backing into a corner with no signs of making an attack."

"Good point. Well on a more positive note, if we can master all of these simulations on ultimate in the next few weeks we should kill it in the arena."

"We'll see," I say as I pick up my shield and go to recover my spear.

"Again?" Clarence asks.

"I'll follow your lead."

We fail that simulation 32 more times over the next three hours before finally calling it a day. Both of us are dragging our feet by the end. I have been shot 14 times, and Clarence 19 times, he calls it rigged every time he gets shot and says he would never get touched if he had a shield like me. There are a few times we think we might actually be able to close it out, but the simulations are too good, and it seems like if we ever try the same thing more than once they are prepared for it and react better the second time. It's as if they learn from our previous attempts how to handle us better each time. My best guess is that the reason for the red lighting is so that the computer can track our movements and use this data to calculate how to best handle us, as well as how best to handle each subsequent attempt. "Well we can't expect to beat it on our first day," I say as we hobble out.

"Yeah," Clarence agrees, "would have been cool though if we did. We are definitely doing this every day, if we master this then the arena will be a piece of cake."

We decide to move on to cardio and stretching before dinner since we still have several hours left in the day. As we exit I look at the computer screen to see if we need to log out or anything, and I notice at the top corner it had a button labeled "Action Report," so I press it. Up pops a summary of each of our 34 matches in the simulator. Each one has total time as well as a report of where we got hit if we did, then at the end it gives suggestions for focus on improvement. Apparently I need to focus on keeping my left shoulder guarded, I was hit eight times in the shoulder, usually when throwing my spear, I was hit three times in the left thigh, one in the right calf, and two times in the left foot. Clarence's report is pretty funny because he got hit literally everywhere, he even took one in the face. That one took a while to recover from. This is good information though, because it's something that we can reference in future sessions in an effort to try and improve.

Clarence pulls the map out and looks for the closest track, which is right next to the weight room. There is a track on each level just like the weights. We take our time walking there in order to regain our composure and energy before we start.

Once we arrive at the track we scan in and I start walking towards the track to start running. Clarence stops me before I can and hands me a 40 pound weight vest. These next few weeks are going to suck.

We start at a slow jog and pick up speed until we are at our normal pace. Running is miserable with the weight vest, it feels as though I can't breathe and my lungs are going to explode, but I persevere. I don't want to be the one quitting and holding Clarence back, if he quits I am totally ready to though. We only run for 30 minutes before calling it quits, apparently Clarence feels it too. The goal is for us to get up to an hour before long, but that feels impossible to me at the moment. Sometimes I feel as though I'm actually allergic to cardio, it makes me all sweaty and clammy and red, and it makes my heart race and I get short on breath. I'm not a doctor, but if you add all that up it can't be healthy.

It's only day one, and I'm already dying, which is depressing since it was a short day. Tomorrow will be death for sure. I just keep telling myself that no matter how hard we work, someone somewhere is working harder, so we have to keep going and keep pushing our limits. I can't see many other people subjecting themselves to this level of punishment.

Clarence and I proceed to take our vests off and walk around for a bit before we decide to move to the middle and stretch. We just do the basics, we don't want to be there for an hour like we would be with yoga. Stretching isn't something we feel we need to do extensively, so long as we do it here and there, but man it feels good after the day we've had. Everything is tight, and everything hurts. I'm dead, and ready to go to bed even though we still have a couple hours before lights out. Taking five days off training was a huge mistake.

We decide it's time for dinner, but need to rinse off first. The shower feels amazing. I just lean against the wall and let the water pour for a few minutes before doing anything else. I needed that. We change into our regular uniforms and head to the cafeteria. When we get there we see a relatively long line, so we have to wait. While we stand there I canvas the room to see how everyone else is looking. For the most part people don't look that tired, there are a few people that look beat, but for the most part people look normal. This is slightly encouraging because it hopefully means that we are going the extra mile while everyone else is following the same old routine. Then again, it is only day one so who knows? The few that look as dead as we are help give me the drive to keep going though, because what happens when we face off against someone who IS working just as hard as we are, or what if they work harder? We need to be ready.

We eventually get our food and hobble over to an empty table as per usual. I don't even pay any attention to what's on my plate, I'm so tired that I really don't care to notice, I just eat it. The food goes down quick, but not too fast since moving seems to take a depressing amount of effort. After we finish we just sit there for a while, neither of us really want to move. We still have two and a half hours before curfew. As we are about to get up we see Joseph and Gordon walking over, they don't look as peppy as usual, but they are nowhere near as destroyed as we are. "How goes it?" Joseph says as they sit down.

"No," I respond, "just no."

"That bad huh?" Joseph says, "You look like you had it pretty rough, must've been a good workout."

"Yes," I say.

"Wow," Gordon says, "we went hard today but apparently not as hard as you guys. Unless you two are just pathetic, in which case we probably did go harder than you."

"Go hard or go home," Clarence says while resting his head on his arm on the table. He's too tired to even care that Gordon is insulting us.

"Apparently," Gordon says, "looks like you guys got ran over by a bus, and then it backed over you and ran you over again."

"At least twice," I say.

"I guess we have to push ourselves a little harder," Joseph says. "If you guys are working hard enough to kill yourselves like this then I bet our workout makes us look weak. Ignore what Gordon said, because I know you guys go hard."

"Did you guys try the combat simulator?" Clarence asks.

"Yeah!" Gordon says, "That thing's pretty fun on beginner! Definitely doing that again tomorrow."

"Yeah try it on ultimate for a few hours and see how good you're feeling afterwards," I say.

"Well that sounds a lot less fun," Gordon says.

"That's because it is less fun," I state.

"Well I think I'm gonna head for the dorm," Clarence says as he slowly rises to his feet. "Gonna study some film and pass out."

"Yeah me too," I say as I struggle to stand up.

"Well have fun boys," Joseph says. "We'll see you in weights tomorrow, sleep well."

"Thanks man, you too," I say as we turn and start to walk away.

"Sleep well ladies," Gordon says with a grin.

"Eat me," Clarence retorts without turning back.

"Maybe later," Gordon says, "I'd rather eat dinner first." We laugh slightly and head out.

Once we get back to the dorm room we turn on the TV to watch some of The Arena, but I fall asleep before the first episode is even over. We have been sleeping on a train for the past week, and we just killed ourselves after not exercising for a week as well. My body needs some quality sleep. I doubt I'll even dream, I just close my eyes and everything shuts off.

Ten hours later my eyes open with the sound of the wake-up call, I'm still tired, but I know we have to get started early. I start to sit up in bed, and the pain sets in. My body is feeling the previous day's workout, everything hurts, and I mean everything. I'm sore in muscles that I haven't felt in a long time. Not sure if it's from a lack of exercise while on tour, or if it's because we pushed ourselves so hard the day before, likely the combination of the two. I just know that today will suck… hard.

V

Every single day we work ourselves half to death. Clarence and I are pushing ourselves to the breaking point. Today will be our final day of training before the games start, and we have no intention of letting up on the intensity.

The wake-up call comes as it always does, I rise immediately and hop off the bunk. "Last day of training," I say to Clarence, who is tying his shoes.

"Make it count," he says as he stands up and high fives me. I'm pumped and ready to go hard, it feels as though with every day that passes we are gaining momentum. Every day I feel better and better, and today I feel great. I quickly change into my weights uniform and we head out.

We are the first ones to scan into the weight room, and we get right to work. Over the past few weeks we have been increasing the intensity in every part of our day, the weight room is no exception. We are no longer taking turns doing sets, now everything is super sets, compound sets, and intermittent cardio between sets. No rest. With every set the goal is complete failure, and when we hit that point we grunt and scream and yell, we don't care if it annoys people, we want everyone to know that we are working harder than them, and we are just getting started.

We are moving onto incline dumbbell bench press when we see Gordon and Joseph walk in, they wave and we wave back. "Last day," Joseph shouts.

"Kill it," I shout back. That's all that's said, they are as determined as we are to get as much done today as possible.

We continue to kill ourselves, just like we do every day. When we finish our workout and start walking towards the exit and I see Gordon and Joseph are doing lat pull-down. "See you guys later," I say as we approach the exit.

"If you don't see us tonight you'll probably see us winning tomorrow!" Gordon says with confidence.

"That's the spirit!" Clarence says enthusiastically.

We are tired from the workout, but we are still driven and we have time to recover during breakfast before we hit the combat simulator. The cafeteria has a line, but it's pretty short. We scan in and out pops super food. Clarence and I requested to be put back on super food after our first few days here, it tastes worse but makes us feel better with regards to energy and recovery. We deemed it a necessary evil. The food goes down, there's no point in taking our time to savor the flavor. We clear our trays and head back to the dorms. We always shower and brush our teeth after breakfast. It seems somewhat pointless since we are going to just get sweaty again shortly thereafter, but we will be disgusting and smelly and probably lose a little respect for ourselves if we don't shower at some point in the morning. Next up is four hours in the combat simulator, so we change into combat uniforms and head out.

Clarence and I approach the first unoccupied room and scan in. We like to begin every day with "Arena Starts" which simulates the start of an arena battle. All arena battles start the same. Combatants meet, unarmed, in the middle of the ring and shake hands as a sign of respect, which is ironic since they are literally about to kill each other. All weapons for every fight are located on the perimeter of the arena in racks on the walls. From there they are placed facing in opposite directions with their heels touching. When the fight commissioner says begin, the battle starts. This is where every combatant must make a choice, you can try to turn and fight your opponent right then and there in hand to hand combat, you can try to knock your opponent over and make a run for the weapons, you can run directly for your weapon of choice, or you can just make a run for whatever is closest to you and try to use that.

The point of this simulation is to prepare you for when you start the battle and have to decide what course of action to take. Generally the least favorable option is the hand to hand combat, because while this one may be quickest, and best for those who are top of their class in hand to hand combat, it is frowned upon by The Arena. To discourage this from happening, there was a rule made so that any match ending in an unsatisfactory amount of time or fashion will result in the prize money being reduced by half. For us that means that if you try to end it quick like that you have to win twice as many matches to earn your freedom. It also means that if you win in a cheap fashion with no honor, such as kicking dirt in your opponents face, you may also lose prize money. Clarence and I prefer to try to get to our weapons and avoid sabotage at the beginning.

The ultimate level for this scenario will try everything in the book, from the simulations sliding their foot back to trip you, to turning and attempting to grapple with you, to turning and just throwing themselves at you. This is essentially a game of tag, and the simulations are it. Clarence and I have developed a strategy that works nearly every time, even against ultimate level simulations. As soon as the simulation yells go, we both jump forward, getting our feet off the ground, and going into a hand spring, while doing so we can look back at the simulations, and depending on their movements we can adjust and either go into a summersault, throw ourselves back into the air and keep going forward, or throw ourselves to either side. The simulations are extremely fast, so we have to be faster, and by this point we are. We have the simulation set to repeat for an hour, the main point of us still doing this is just developing muscle memory for when the real deal comes. They say it takes 10,000 hours to master something, well we don't have that long so we figure 10,000 runs through the simulation will suffice. The only time we ever fail the simulation is if we have stupid mistakes such as slipping, or hitting each other every now and again if our simulations' movements cause us to spring towards one another. By the time our hour is up my shoulders are on fire, doing shoulders in the gym and then following up with hand springs for an hour is killer, but necessary. Next we move onto hand to hand combat.

The hand to hand combat simulator is different from the rest, because it raises two pillars out of the ground with a dozen two-foot long handles sticking out of it. These handles are all mechanized and can rotate around the body, or extend from the body, according to commands given by the computer. The key here is to not only block attempts that it makes to hit you, but to try and hit the main body, which it will try and block with the handles. There's no winning or losing in this exercise, only positive and negative responses by the machine. If you successfully hit the body it lights up green, for every time the machine hits your torso or head it will light up red. Clarence and I spend thirty minutes sparring with the dummies, and then we spar with each other.

I hate sparring with Clarence, because he's just better than me at hand to hand combat, he always has been, so he will kick my butt nine times out of ten. In the few instances where I manage to put him into submission it feels pretty good though. Even though I hate it, I appreciate it because I'm getting more out of it than he is. You get more out of trying to overcome someone better than you, than you do fighting someone lesser than yourself. The times where I did beat him however, he always grins and gets more excited about it. It's not like I'm that much worse than he is, we were both in the top of our class for hand to hand combat, but he still makes me look bad more often than not. I'm feeling pumped today though, and when we get to sparring I'm determined to take him down, which I do. I manage to take him down in our first bout with a sweeping kick into an arm bar. While an arm bar might not be deadly in a real fight, people tend to have a harder time if you break their arm, at least that's the theory. "Looks like someone is extra fired up today," Clarence says. "You actually got me."

"Gotta go hard on the last day. No exceptions."

"That's good, too bad it isn't going to happen again." And it doesn't. For the next 25 or so minutes Clarence cleaned my clock. He put me into just about every possible submission, which I think was his plan. I still feel pretty good about getting him once though. Once we finish sparring it's time to move onto melee combat. We select our usual weapons of choice and head towards the middle.

For melee combat the computer will spawn simulations with various melee weapons from swords, to spears, to flails, to axes, nothing is off limits. At ultimate level the simulations are ridiculous, they will attack with unending ferocity and power to keep you on the defensive, and they are agile enough to dodge nearly all of your attacks. It's good that the simulations are so intense, because it will be hard for any human to come at us as hard and fast as the simulations do. There's no surefire way to beat this simulation, but it makes us better fighters overall, and we manage to win the majority of bouts at this point. We have discovered that rather than blocking their attacks it's better to dodge them if possible, so we have become much faster over the three weeks. Clarence has figured out ways to disarm his attacker by pinching their weapon between his swords and leveraging it out of their hands. He has also developed a technique where if he managed to dodge them he would drop a scimitar and grab their weapon while swinging his other sword down on their arm.

I on the other hand have become more reliant on my shield the more we do it, I dodge what I can, and absorb the rest, and when the opportunity presents itself I bash the simulation with my shield and follow up with an attack from my spear. We have also gotten really good at watching each other's simulations with our peripheral vision, and if we see openings we assist each other. One of our most effective strategies involves me waiting for an opportunity to shove my opponent off with my shield, and while they are off balance I turn and throw my spear at Clarence's opponent, while my spear is coming Clarence will always attack from another direction, there's almost no way to dodge the spear and block Clarence at the same time. Techniques like this will definitely come in handy in the arena.

Feedback from the computer also helped us to improve our defensive tactics, Clarence has become better at defending his feet, which he hadn't given much thought to before he was stabbed a couple dozen times in the simulator. And I have gotten better at protecting my back and left shoulder, the simulator quickly taught me that I can't rely on Clarence to literally cover my back every fight, nor can I ignore his simulation. We manage to win every single bout for the first time ever, it feels good. It feels right too, since it's the last day and we need to win every bout to feel as confident as possible going into the fight tomorrow. Now all that's left to do is projectile training.

Projectile training is the first one that we managed to master, we figured if it was the one we started with it should be the first one we finish. We have gotten to the point that we are tracking the number of arrows that we block before even considering an offensive move. The simulations have unlimited arrows, but in the arena each quiver of arrows only contains 50 arrows, so in theory if we block 50 in the simulation the archer will be out of ammunition in real life. We have seen many episodes of the arena where an archer will use all 50 arrows and then panic trying to get to another quiver, and that's usually when they lose.

Once we have each counted to 50 arrows, we then start maneuvering around. Clarence takes a speed approach in that he will strafe back and forth while running as fast as he can towards the archer. Over the three weeks of practicing he has gotten really good at cutting arrows out of the air, so he just deflects anything that comes his way as he makes his way to the archer and cuts them down. I just go full turtle mode and move opposite Clarence while slowly closing the gap, so if my archer turns for Clarence I can make my move, or if it focuses on me Clarence can dispatch it after he deals with his.

Projectiles has managed to become another simulation that's more for getting in as many attempts as possible before game day, rather than for actual difficulty. Neither of us have been hit by a single arrow in almost a week, it's just practice now. With how accurate and mobile the simulations are, we feel confident that we can handle archers if we have to. We are finishing strong as far as the simulator goes, it makes me wonder how many others have bested the simulator. I doubt it's very many, but I know we won't be the only ones.

Once we've done projectiles for an hour Clarence and I rack our weapons and exit. "Great job in there today man," I say to Clarence.

"You too man," He responds. "I'm tellin' you, we are the dynamic duo. Nothin' gonna stop us once we get out there."

"Let's not get ahead of ourselves. Simulations are just simulations, the real deal will be way more intense and have a lot more factors to play on."

"I know, but we got this, I can feel it."

We make our way to the cafeteria for lunch, super food again. We get our trays, find an empty table, and eat. With every meal I just keep telling myself that I will only have to stomach this stuff until we win our first match, and then I will be able to go back on the good stuff. Part of me knows I'm lying to myself though, because we will always have another match to train for. I wish I could have real food and train as hard as we are, but it just isn't the same. I can honestly feel the difference between regular food and super food as soon as I eat it. It's a depressing truth. No matter how much it saddens my taste buds, it isn't going to kill the momentum that I have going today. I'm feeling good, motivated, driven. Cardio here we come.

We clear our trays, then leave the cafeteria and make our way to the track. We have developed a ridiculously intense training regimen for cardio. Both of us barely manage to walk out every single day. First we start with weight free sprints. We sprint the straits of the track and jog the curves. Next we put wrist weights on to mimic the weight of our weapons. Then we do the sprint routine again. After we do that for a mile we just jog five miles with the wrist weights. Next up we grab the weight vests. Once we have those we do the same thing, sprint the straits and jog the curves for a mile followed by another five-mile jog. The idea is that if we can run fast with this much extra weight on us we should be able to run even faster without it. It's also good for endurance training to make sure we didn't tire out in the middle of a fight. Finally once we have done our running with the weighted vests we ditch all of the weights and grab a running parachute and do one more mile with the parachute to really destroy whatever we have left to destroy and increase our speed.

We gradually progressed up to this point over the first two weeks, and then started doing this routine for the final week. I'm not ashamed to say that I have collapsed on multiple occasions, and thrown up three times. Clarence is in the same boat, but he only ever puked once. All of this takes a couple hours. Time for mobility training. For this we go to the center of the arena inside the track and start stretching out.

Mobility training takes roughly an hour, we are very thorough. Originally we only planned to do it here and there, but by day three we realized that we were just being lazy and decided to man up and do it every day. We have a routine that we go through twice, holding each stretch for two minutes.

After completing our stretches I feel pretty good, I'm still destroyed on some level, but an hour of recovery goes a long ways. We have managed to get all of our training done for the day, now all that's left is dinner, but we don't want to eat yet since we still have six hours left in our day, so we head back to our dorm to shower and change into our regular uniforms. After showering we decide to watch TV for an hour before eating to be as prepped as possible, we have seen every episode a million times, aside from those that aired recently, but you can never study too much. Plus we have plans with Gordon and Joseph to eat around 5:30pm if possible.

We don't want to train anymore because we want to be recovered and ready for tomorrow, plus there's nothing left to do really. When we first developed this routine at the start of the three weeks, it literally took us all day, but as we pushed ourselves harder and harder we've managed to condense it down to just ten hours. I feel pretty good about it, in those ten hours we push ourselves harder than most everyone else we see training. It's crazy to think how far we've come in just three weeks. All our lifts have increased significantly. We have each gained over five pounds of muscle. We have managed to take a 16 hour workout and condense it to 10 hours while still progressively increasing the intensity each day. We have done what seemed impossible on day one and beat every core simulation on ultimate, as well as a few of the more fine-tuned ones such as "Arena Starts." We're ready for this, I know we are.

After the hour has finally passed, we motivate ourselves to get up and go to dinner. "Can't have Gordon crying if we don't show up," I say as we walk out.

"Yeah," Clarence agrees, "we would never hear the end of it."

"I'd never tell him, but I actually want to see them one last time before tomorrow, a last hurrah and good luck before everyone has to fight, you know?"

"Same here man," Clarence says.

VI

The cafeteria is packed when we get there, we have to wait in line for quite a while. Eventually we get scanned and get our trays as per usual, but as we are looking for an empty table something changes. For the first time ever, Joseph and Gordon are actually at a table waiting for us to sit down. I can't believe it. "Saved you a seat," Joseph smiles as we walk over and sit down.

"I'm shocked," I say. "I guess there's a first time for everything."

"What do you mean?" Gordon asks, "We always beat you guys here, in fact I would be impressed if you ever managed to get here before us." Sometimes I wonder if he really does live in his own world.

"Is that so?" Clarence asks, "Well if that's the case I apologize for being such a pig and finishing my food before you every time. Even though you supposedly get here first."

"Apology accepted," Gordon says. "I understand, it's just in your nature to be a disgusting pig when it comes to food, and I can live with that so long as you can." Everyone laughs and shakes their head at Gordon and his nonsense.

"Do you plan out talking points for the day every morning, or does it just come to you and you spout it out on the fly?" I ask.

"Oh this is all on the go," Gordon says, "It just so happens that I'm not only ridiculously attractive, but smart as well."

"Or you're just crazy," Clarence says, "because you are anything but handsome bud."

"Ouch," Joseph says, "let me go grab some ice for that, because you're going to need it."

"I'm good actually," Gordon says, "some people just can't help but project their qualities onto those that they find threatening. It's sad really."

"Oh so you're a psychologist now?" Clarence asks.

"I'm whatever I need to be, whenever I need to be it," Gordon responds.

"Well then maybe you need to sit down and have a conversation with yourself, cause you've got issues," Clarence says.

"Sure you don't need that ice?" Joseph asks.

"No, but I'll take some ointment if you have it," Gordon says.

"Wait what?" I ask, "Since when does Gordon just back down like that? You feeling alright buddy?"

"I figured I should let Clarence have this one win in honor of the eve of our impending victories," Gordon states.

"Well that was awfully nice of you," Joseph says.

"Why thank you," Clarence says mockingly, "I just can't imagine how I ever would have won that argument had you not conceded, you're just so smart and witty, much smarter than I."

"Yeah yeah," Gordon says, "Enjoy it while it lasts, because next time I'm going to make you wish you were deaf."

"You do that almost every time you open your mouth bud," Clarence says.

"AND THE BURNS KEEP COMING!" Joseph shouts.

"Like I said, enjoy it while you can," Gordon states.

Everyone is finishing up eating at this point, it's weird to think that I'm actually sad to be done eating. Usually I'm happy to be done, but this time it's different. This is the last time that we are all guaranteed to be together. No one wants to say it out loud, but I'm sure that everyone is thinking it. I look around the table and everyone is forcing halfhearted smiles with hollow eyes. We are all nervous about tomorrow, not just for ourselves, but for our friends. What would life be without your friends, I can't imagine losing any one of the guys at this table, I just have to keep my chin up and be enthusiastic. Every match needs a winner right? "Before we go," I say, "I just want to say good luck to everyone tomorrow. We have all put in a lot of hard work over the past few weeks, and it all leads up to tomorrow's fights. I expect everyone to give it 100% tomorrow, and if your best isn't good enough, then do the best of someone better. I will tolerate no losses tomorrow and expect to see everyone for dinner tomorrow, or else I'm gonna kick your asses, got it?"

"Got it!" Everyone says at the same time with a smile. We are all hollow inside at this point, or at least filled with uncertainty, but no one will let it show. "Group hug?" Joseph asked.

"Alright, but you guys better not touch my voluptuous booty," Gordon says.

"As if anyone would want to," Clarence says.

We exchange a quick laugh and everyone comes in for a group hug at the end of the table before leaving. "Hey guys," I say. "Don't say goodbye, just see you later."

"See you later!," Joseph says as he turns to leave with his usual heartwarming smile.

"Later ladies," Gordon says as he follows Joseph.

"See ya boys," Clarence says.

"I'll see you guys later…" I say as the two of them walk out.

I could feel a weird feeling coming over me, it's like a strong anxiety brought on by the uncertainty of tomorrow's events. I can't let it get to me though, I can't afford to worry about Joseph's or Gordon's fight, I have my own fight to worry about. I'm going to see Joseph smile again, and hear Gordon make a fool of himself again, but in order to do that I have to win my own fight tomorrow. All that's left to do now is watch some TV and get some sleep, tomorrow is going to be the biggest day of my life thus far, and its go big or die trying. Literally.

VII

Today is the day. The day everyone will be put to the ultimate test. Today we enter the arena, and show the world what we're made of. Clarence and I are ready, at least as ready as we can be. We have been training diligently with the sole purpose of making it through today. I just have to keep telling myself that. *We're ready. We can do this. I can do this.*

The 6am wakeup call comes just as it always does, but I'm already awake. I haven't started to get ready yet, but I've been lying in bed for the past half hour or so just staring at the ceiling trying to stay positive. "Let's go, big day," Clarence says. I guess that means it's time for me to get ready.

There's a knock at the door, Clarence opens it to reveal an orderly. This is just like the morning of the start of the preseason tour. "Train leaves in thirty minutes, don't be late." He says, and he's gone. I hop down from the top bunk and grab a towel, time to hit the showers since we won't have a morning workout. After showering and brushing my teeth I put on my regular uniform. "What are you waiting for?" I ask Clarence, "Let's go."

"My man!" We walk out the door and start making our way towards the entrance of the facility.

There is a short line at the entrance, people are scanning in and boarding. Everyone knows the drill from last time. Clarence and I scan in, seats 121 and 122 again. We board, we sit, and we wait. Before long the doors close and the intercom comes on, "Good morning everyone, we shall soon depart for The Arena headquarters. Upon arrival you will scan again and be assigned a color, red group shall follow the orderly on the left, and blue group shall follow the orderly on the right. The purpose of this sorting is to prevent intermingling of opponents. Once everyone is sorted you shall be guided to a locker room where you shall change into your attire for the day. From there you shall be escorted to a waiting room which has food you may enjoy while you wait. All combatants shall be called to their final waiting room when the match preceding theirs is about to begin, from there you will be told when to enter the arena. That is all." Once the intercom cuts out the train starts to move.

My whole life has led up to this day, and to be honest I thought I would be more nervous than I am. Maybe it's the training, maybe it's that Clarence is with me, or maybe it just hasn't set in yet, but so far I feel calm and ready. I have a clear mind, my hands are steady, and my heart beat is calm. Just a couple of hours left.

The train ride really is short, only a few minutes, but I guess that's because we are just moving from the outskirts of the city to the center, rather than across the country. The train stops, and the doors open. I see light, but I don't get my hopes up. If every other train ride ended inside, this one won't be any different. I still have hopes of seeing the outside world, but my hopes of seeing the sky before entering the arena have all but died. As we exit the train my suspicions are confirmed, it's just another train terminal with a scanner waiting for us, and two orderlies on either side of the terminal. This terminal is a lot less fancy than the others, it's just cement. Everything is big and open, but it's all cement. We must be below the arena. I guess there is really no point in making things look pretty when half of the people passing through here will be dead by the end of the day.

Clarence and I scan just like everyone else as we exit the train, we get blue so we walk to the right. There is a small wait, but once everyone has scanned the orderlies turn and start walking, and everyone follows. I look around and see that there's not too many people here, only about 150 guys total, they must have only brought those who are likely to fight today. I see Gordon walking away with the red group, he looks serious and doesn't notice me at all, but I don't see Joseph anywhere, maybe he isn't fighting today. The entire walk is dull and feels like the cold depressing walk of doom rather than an uplifting morale boosting walk towards victory.

The locker room is more cement with giant metal cubbies. "Your locker numbers are the same as your seat numbers, you have ten minutes to change," the orderly says after everyone has entered the room. Clarence and I make our way to lockers 121 and 122.

"Hey look," Clarence says, "Real clothes! Kind of."

"That sucks, I was hoping we would get to fight in our underwear."

"Yeah me too, but I will say these were my second pick." He says as he holds up his loincloth.

Our outfits for the arena are modeled after traditional gladiators from ancient Rome, all leather with a metal shoulder pad. We are supplied with knee high strapped leather sandals, leather bracers for our forearms, a leather loincloth that is barely more concealing than the speedos, and a metal shoulder pad strapped across our torsos. It's basic, but this is just our first fight. The more fights you win the more armor they give you. I look around and see

107

that there are various shades of brown and black leather for everyone, I guess that way we don't all look the same to the audience. Clarence and I got dark black leather. We each change and then check ourselves out. We look amazing, at least I think we do. Everything is tight though, and a little uncomfortable. "If people didn't love us in the preseason tour, they are sure to love us when they see us lookin' like this," Clarence says.

"You're welcome."

"Yeah like they will even notice you with me out there."

"We'll see."

The ten minutes we were given pass by quickly, "Follow me to the waiting room," the orderly says, "There you will wait until you are called up to head to the final waiting room before your match. There will be food there, you may eat as much, or as little, as you want." With that he turns and starts to walk away, and again we all follow him. Looking around I notice that a lot of the guys are walking funny, or adjusting their clothing, at least I'm not the only one who is uncomfortable in this stuff.

It's a short walk to the waiting room, only a couple minutes. When we get there the orderly waits for everyone to enter, and then he closes the doors behind us. The waiting room is a little nicer, and rather spacious, which makes sense since there are about 75 of us waiting. The floors are black mats like most of our combat classes, which is nice compared to cement, and the walls are still cement but they have motivational posters of various champions with sayings like "Fight like there's no tomorrow." Ironic. It would have been more uplifting had the posters been in the hallways on the walk over though, at least that's what I think. There are black cloth couches lining the walls and matching chairs all around the room with a white table in the center which is loaded with various meats, fruits, and vegetables. At the end of the table there is a platter of super food as well. My stomach is screaming for me to dive into all the delicious food, but this isn't the time to cave to desires, I have to remain focused on the task at hand. I grab some super food. On the far wall of the room there is a massive projection covering the entire wall, on it is 'The Arena', this must be so that we can all watch today's matches while we wait. There is also a large digital clock in the top left corner of the screen. It reads 7:30, if memory serves that means we have 30 minutes until the first match of the season takes place. The first day of every season starts at 8am and the show goes until 8pm, it stays this way for the entire week until everyone has had their first match. Then from there they tone it back to an hour of matches every day.

"Breakfast time!" Clarence says as he walks over to the table and puts some super food on a plate.

"How can you be excited for that stuff?"

"Gotta put some fuel in the tank if I want to be at my best, you should do the same man."

"I know, I was just saying how can you be excited for it? I'll eat it, but I'll never celebrate doing so, unless they have starved me for a few days."

"Gotta keep your head up! GAME DAY BABY!" He is so over the top excited for this, I don't get it. Maybe it's just his way of avoiding thinking about how scary it really is. Or maybe he's just that confident, I mean we are one percenters according to the tour, and we've come a long ways since then.

"Yeah I guess. Oh yay super paste!" I say half-cheerily as I put some on a plate. Neither of us grabbed that much since it's possible that we would be one of the very first matches. The first day of every season starts with four diamond one matches, and the final four matches of the week will also be diamond one. It's like an opening and closing ceremony of sorts, the rest of the matches are varying skill levels but it always rotates around the four types: guy singles, girl singles, guy doubles, and girl doubles. We proceed to sit down at a couch close to the screen, that way we can see the first matches as well as keep track of the time.

"Theon," An orderly says from the entrance, "Follow me to the final waiting room please. As the orderly said it a huge man started walking towards the door. *Wow, there's no way that guy is our age is there? He's a monster, he makes me look small.* Theon has to be at least 6'6" tall weighing well over 200lbs with a shaved head and a fierce look on his face.I feel bad for whoever has to face that guy, I would be scared if that was the guy I had to fight, I mean seriously that guy is massive.

"Wow," Clarence says.

"I know. I feel for whoever he's fighting."

"Never know, size isn't everything man."

"Yeah, but it doesn't hurt."

"Plus if you look at it like this, sure that guy is a freak of nature, but I bet that huge body makes him super slow. Someone who is quick on his feet could dance circles around him."

"I guess we'll see here shortly."

"Sure will, now eat your food, we could be up any time." Clarence is super focused, I wish I knew what was really going through his head. Is he actually super calm, prepped, and ready for this? Or is he a little nervous like me? I eat my super food and wash it down with some water, waiting for the show to start.

Finally at 8:00am sharp the screen changes, and the opening credits for The Arena begin. I've seen it a million times, but this time is different, this time I'll be fighting. The screen goes dark, there is an eerie slow music that starts so quiet you can barely hear it, then it progressively builds becoming louder and louder. A fire appears in the distance with one man dressed in combatant apparel standing on the far side of it, surrounded by darkness. "What makes a legend?" A deep gruff voice says, his voice is almost a growl. "Is a legend born?" A clash of swords flashes across the screen. "Is it heroic acts that make a legend?" Two men in a struggle flash on screen. "Or is it hard work and blood shed takes a man and forges

110

him into legend?" It shows a man standing covered in blood holding his sword high in the air in the middle of the arena. "Legends are not born, they are not heroes, they are champions immortalized by fiery crucible of combat!" The camera is right next to the man by the fire now, he is looking down into the flames. "Who will answer the call of the arena? Who will rise…to become… legend?" As the voice says legend the man by the fire suddenly looks up and stares straight into the camera with a fierce look across his face. Shivers go down my spine.

The camera then cuts to two men sitting in the shout casters' box with the arena in the background. "Hello everyone, and welcome to another exciting season of 'The Arena', I'm Charles Platt and alongside me is Blake Lewis."

"Today we bring you a new batch of combatants fresh from the academy, and let me tell you from what I've seen on the preseason tour this season will be one of the best yet."

"Now as always this week is First Blood Week in the arena, that means that everyone will be fighting for the first time. And when I say everyone, I mean EVERYONE that is coming into the arena this season will be fighting for the first time. And we will have it all live right here from 8am until 8pm pacific standard time."

"You know Charles, people ask me every year if I ever get tired of casting during First Blood Week, and you know what I tell them?"

"What's that Blake?"

"I tell them, how can you ever get sick of seeing gladiators battling it out for the first time ever? I tell them it may be 12 hours a day, but it doesn't feel like it. Like much of the world, I love the sport and I never miss a fight."

"Couldn't have said it better myself. You know Blake I remember the feeling I had the first time I watched a match, it was so exhilarating my hands started to tremble. I knew from that day that I was going to love this sport and that there wasn't a place I would rather be than right here…" I really couldn't care less for the back and forth banter they have every day before the fights start, and in between the fights as well. It's the same every time, they talk about a little history and interacting with the fans, then they finally talk about the gladiators that are about to fight, and then it gets interesting when the fight actually starts. I feel like their commentating and quick wits add to the show. Blake especially is super quick tongued, I have no idea how he comes up with some of the stuff he says but it adds to the moment, whether he is trying to add to the seriousness of the moment or making a comical remark about what just happened. However, I find it disgusting how into it they get when they've never had their lives on the line like we do.

Clarence and I sit down on a couch close to the screen, I could care less for the pre-fight show but I want to be close to see the first fight as clearly as possible. "Here we go baby!" Clarence yells. I pay attention to the screen again, they are starting to talk about the first match.

"Blake it looks like we are going to see some pretty amazing action here in this first match of the day, featuring fighters Theon and Gordon. What are your thoughts about these two combatants?" Wait what? Did he just say Gordon? Gordon is fighting that freak beast of a man that just walked out of this room? This can't be happening.

"Well Charles, I saw them on the preseason tour and let me tell you, this Theon guy is one tough cookie. He is number one in his class in weights and weapons training. Standing at six foot six and 260 lbs he is a muscle monster the likes of which this doesn't see too often. His opponent Gordon on the other hand, doesn't have much going for him. He was in the middle of his class in all areas the past year, stands six feet tall and only 180 lbs. I just don't see how this kid stands a chance against an animal like Theon, but who knows maybe he will surprise us. He did get diamond one after all, although I'm not sure how."

"When you put it like that I would hate to be in Gordon's shoes right now. You are right though, there is always the long shot that he will have something up his sleeve to beat the odds, an ace in the hole if you will."

"It looks like we're about to find out Charles, because here they come! The first match of the day, Theon versus Gordon, winner take all."

"Don't worry man," Clarence says calm and collected, "Gordon's got this, he's too stubborn to die." I really hope Clarence is right, because I'm freaking out a little bit. I can barely sit still, I'm at the edge of my seat with anticipation. This is literally worst case scenario for Gordon. He has to win though, he has to.

The camera cuts from the shout casters to the arena. Intense battle drums start to play as two doors on opposite sides of the arena open to reveal Theon and Gordon. They each look so serious, I don't know that I've ever seen Gordon this serious before. As they made their way to the center of the arena the drums progressively pick up the pace until the two finally meet in the middle and the beat climaxes and dies in an instant. They each stand in the center of the arena for a moment staring at each other, it looks like you can fit two of Gordon inside Theon, what a beast. They shake hands and turn around back to back. Now they get into a slight lunge and put the heel of their back foot against one another. It's about to begin, my heart is racing and I almost want to throw up. I'm depressingly anxious for someone else's fight, hopefully this doesn't happen when I'm out there. What am I thinking? Am I really thinking about my fight when one of my best friends is about to fight for his life? I'm so self-centered... *Come on Gordon!*

"LET'S GO!" Clarence screams and claps his hands. Several of the other guys in the room cheer with Clarence, I think they are just cheering for the show in general though.

"Here we go," Blake starts on screen, "The calm before the storm, the silence before the battle, the beginning of the end for one and the chance to seize glory for another. Who will emerge victorious? Let's find out! In 3...2...1... FIGHT!" The match begins.

As soon as the match starts Gordon immediately goes up on the balls of his feet and rotates around as Theon starts to try and run away. Gordon then immediately throws himself onto the back of Theon, wrapping his legs around his torso and putting him into a rear naked choke while tucking his head down. I can't believe it. "YEAH!" Clarence screams as he jumps up, "GET HIM GORDON GET HIM!"

"I don't know what's happening," Charles says, "It would appear as though Gordon is trying to end this match as soon as it starts."

"Looks as though Theon isn't going to go down easy though," Blake says as Theon starts hitting Gordon all over his body and on top of his head, but Gordon doesn't let go.

"I'm not sure what's more impressive, the fact that Gordon is taking such a beating without letting go, or that Theon is able to throw out so many punches without being able to breathe."

Theon keeps hitting Gordon over and over, but Gordon never lets go. Slowly after what seems like forever, but in reality is only a little over a minute or so, Theon starts to wobble and stagger step. He finally stops punching, and finally falls over, landing right on top of Gordon, but Gordon keeps his choke hold.

"I'm awestruck, I just simply don't believe it, Theon is down and out." Charles says.

"Looks like lights out for the monster, is this the end?" Blake adds. It bothers me slightly how surprised and seemingly saddened the announcers are that Gordon is winning. Literally no one except Clarence and I are rooting for him.

Gordon finally releases his grip and struggles to roll Theon off of him. The crowd is silent, the room we are in is silent. He

114

slowly makes his way to his feet, his body is bruised all over, but not broken. Slowly regaining his composure he slowly walks over towards the edge of the arena, Theon is on the ground lifeless, it's hard to tell if he is still breathing or not. Gordon finally makes it to the wall and grabs a battle axe. He drops the head of the axe to the ground and holds it by the base of the handle with one hand as he turns and slowly starts walking back to Theon.

"I don't know if I can even watch this," Charles says, "David is about to crush Goliath in front of millions of people and there is nothing Goliath can do to defend himself. The number one contender going into the season is moments away from being taken out by a seemingly inferior competitor."

Gordon finally reaches Theon and stops, standing near his shoulders. He lets out a sigh and slings the axe up over his shoulder. Grabbing it with both hands he raises it up above his head and brings it down right onto Theon's neck, severing his head from his body. Gordon doesn't even remove the axe from the dirt in which its head is stuck. He just stands up and throws his arms up in the air with the smirk that we see daily. "WOOOOO!" He yells at the crowd, which is still silent.

"Well there you have it folks," Blake says, "The long shot manages to pull through after all. Gordon Immerges victorious, and Theon pays the ultimate price in the arena."

It takes me a second to process what had just happened, Gordon did it, he won. "He actually did it," I say.

"I TOLD YOU!" Clarence says, "There's no way my man is gonna go out in the first round! WOO!" Clarence is grinning from ear to ear, his grin is even bigger than Gordon's is on the TV. I'm smiling too, it's a relief knowing that there is one less fried to worry about.

"One opponent down, four to go."

"Four to go? Don't you mean three? There's our fight and then my man Joseph is gonna tear it up tomorrow or whenever it is he's fighting."

"Kayleah too."

"Oh! That's right! I wasn't thinking about Dime, I guess that does make it four more then huh?"

"Yeah, we are 20% of the way to achieving our goal, at least for this week."

"This week, next week, every week! Nothing can stop us! The pain train is only gonna pick up momentum all the way to the finish line!"

"You're right, we got this no sweat right?" I know I need to try to be more optimistic and keep my mind off of everything with our fight coming up soon.

"That's right!"

Gordon finally exits the arena leaving the silent crowd behind him. "Well I can't say it was good fight, but a fight it was indeed. However, since Gordon did finish Theon off so quickly, and in a less than exciting fashion, he will be penalized and only receive half the credits." Charles states. *Screw you Charles.*

"That's the one downside to ending things quick like that," Blake adds, "the people want to see a good fight and if you don't give it to them and end it early, you leave with a smaller paycheck." *Screw you too Blake.*

"Well one fight down, and many more to go. We're going to take a quick break to clean up the carnage, but when we get back we have another amazing match-up between the number one singles female contender Kayleah and her opponent Rose! Stay tuned!" And with that it cut to commercial.

"What?" I ask.

"Oh man," Clarence says.

"This can't be happening, how is she the second fight?"

"Hey man I'm sure she's gonna be fine, they just said she's literally the best."

"Yeah but look how that ended up for Theon."

"Hey! I need you to focus up right now, we have a fight here soon and I need you thinking about that and not her. You can worry about her later."

"At least we get to watch it like Gordon's I guess, I just didn't expect her fight to be so soon." I may be more nervous about her fight than I am about our fight.

"Yeah man, she's gonna do great just wait and see."

We hear the door open as the broadcast resumes. "Welcome back to The Arena!" Charles says with energy.

"Clarence and Royce, this way please," a voice calls from the entrance. This can't be happening, not now, not when Kayleah is about to fight. Literally any other time and I will happily go, just not now. My heart hits the floor and my body feels like it weighs a million pounds, I have no will to move, but I don't have a choice. We are being called to the final waiting room.

"I know it sucks man, but we gotta go and you need to focus up." Clarence says as he stands and grabs my shoulder.

"Hopefully they have the broadcast in the other room too," I say enthusiastically.

"I'm sure they do man, let's go." I start to stand and follow Clarence to the door where the orderly is standing. As we exit the room I look back over my shoulder and see Kayleah walking out onto the arena. I only see her for a second, in her leather attire and metal shoulder pad with her hair back in a ponytail. She has a fierce piercing stare on her face, she looks determined and ready. The door

117

closes, and she's gone. The walk to the final waiting room is short, and all I can think about on the way there is her. This is killing me inside because I want so badly for her to not have to fight at all. I wish there was a way I could just fight for her, or rather double my win requirement so she can just walk free. I want so badly to be able to carry this weight for her, at least that way I know she's safe and I don't have to worry about her. Honestly I wish I could do that for all of my friends to keep them safe, if I had to win 100 matches so my friends could all see their freedom and never have to enter the arena I would, but I want that for Kayleah more than anything. In my heart I know she can do this. *She has to do this.* She will do this. *I hope she does it.*

The orderly opens a door and stands next to it gesturing with his hand for us to enter. "Wait here until it's time for your match," The orderly says, when it's your time the door will open, and you will enter the arena."

We step inside and the room is fairly dark, dimly lit by a small red light in the cement ceiling above us. There is no screen with the broadcast in sight. "Is there any way we can watch this match?" I ask the orderly before he leaves.

"The final waiting room is intended to be an isolated room for the combatants to gather their thoughts and strategies in preparation for their match, no outside influences or distractions before the fight." The orderly responds, and then he shuts the door without another word.

"Man I'm sorry, but like I said she'll be fine and we need to focus up alright?" Clarence says.

"This is just my luck, but you're right, I can't worry about her. She's gotta fight her own battles and I have to fight mine, time to get pumped up and ready."

"There we go!"

118

And now the wait begins. The longest, and yet shortest, wait of my life. The wait before the fight that decides if we live or die, if I see my friends again or not, if I see Kayleah again or not. I will see her again. *I have to see her again.* I'm going to see her again.

VIII

"Time to focus up," Clarence says as we sit on benches on opposite sides of the dim lit final waiting room. "Gather your thoughts, do what you gotta do, but when that door opens and it's our time to shine I need you out there with me. I can't do this alone."

I may have a lot of stressors in the back of my mind right now, but I know that he's right, and I know that I can't take all of my mental baggage out onto the battlefield with me. I can worry about everyone else later, right now I just need to worry about us and what lies ahead. "Don't worry, I'm good."

"Just remember, we worked our butts off to get to this point, and there's nothing that the two guys waiting for us can do to stop us. We're the top dogs around here, and we have to show the world that we're here to stay. You with me?"

"Always."

"That's what I like to hear." Under different circumstances Clarence could have made a living as a motivational speaker if he had the opportunity. He always seems to know what to say to get my head in the game.

No more words are spoken after that, we just sit and wait in silence. I do my best to clear my head and focus on what's about to happen and go through all of our training in my head. I know that once I get out there and the fight starts that adrenaline, instinct, and muscle memory will kick in and I will probably forget a lot of this, but I need to do something to prepare myself.

It's a strange concept now that I think about it, but Clarence and I are literally about to fight two other people to the death, and I'm decently calm all things considered. I thought that I would get the jitters and be super nervous, but I'm fairly relaxed for being a few minutes away from the big event. Maybe things will change once we get out there and have to stand in front of everyone and the fight is actually happening, or maybe it won't, no sense in worrying about it I guess. I also find it surprising how quiet this room is, we are only a few feet away from the edge of the arena, and I'm assuming we are directly under the crowd, but I can't hear anything except for the sound of Clarence and I breathing; they did a good job sound proofing this room. I guess it makes sense though, it would probably be distracting if we could hear every sound the crowd makes in reaction to the current fight.

Finally after a decent amount of time has passed, though it's hard to say how much because we are left to our own devices in this room, a rumble is heard and the large doors to the arena start to open. Clarence and I make eye contact as soon as we hear the doors start to move. We both rise to our feet, "Here we go," I say.

"Show time, let's do this," he says as he smacks me on the shoulder. "Here we go baby! Time to show the world what a real doubles team looks like!"

"LET'S DO IT!" I yell back. We both start to jump around some and warm up, my heartbeat is starting to rise. This is really happening, there's no turning back (not that there ever was). The doors take about 30 seconds to open, which gives the announcers time to ramble on about the contenders that are about to enter the arena.

The noise is subtle at first, but the more the doors open the louder and louder the crowd and the announcers get. When the doors are finally open all the way I can hear the announcers' voices, "CLARENCE AAAANNNNDDDD ROYCE!" That must be our queue. Here we go.

Clarence and I both step out into the light, which is almost blinding at first after having been in darker room for a while. We both walk with confidence, throwing our arms up in the air and gesturing towards the crowd. This is more Clarence's style than mine, but I know we need to try to make a good impression. The more the crowd likes us the more beneficial it will be to us in the future. We slowly make our way to the center of the arena, turning various directions as we walk trying to play the crowd as much as possible. I'm not sure what the announcers said about us while we were still in the room, but it must have been good because the crowd seems to be as pumped up as we are for the ensuing fight. As I look to the center of the arena I see two guys already standing there waiting for us.

I recognize them from seeing them around the academy over the years, but I can't say that I know them. I've never had any classes that I can think of with either of them. We finally get to the middle of the arena and pause for a moment to size one another up. One is decently tall, roughly 6'3" I'd say, with very short bright orange hair, blue eyes, and freckles all over his pale body. He's decently built, but still rather slender looking for his height, he has a fierce look in his eyes with pronounced cheek bones and a pointed jaw. His body may not be intimidating, but his glare tells me that he means business. His partner is much smaller than he is, only about

121

5'8" with short dark brown hair, brown eyes, and a light brown skin complexion. The partner seems softer than he is, with a rounded face and chubby cheeks that don't match his hardened body. He too possesses a stern look on his face, it just doesn't have the same effect as his taller friend though. No one says a word, we all just stand there for a moment and stare at each other, and once that moment has passed we exchange handshakes. It's weird to think that you are either shaking the hand of the person you are about to kill, or the person who is about to kill you. A sign of respect, but none the less a strange sentiment in my opinion. After we all shake hands we all turn our backs on one another and enter our ready positions with our heels touching in the dead center of the arena, turning our bodies into a giant "X". There's an awkward pause now, all of us ready and just waiting to hear the words. Waiting for the shout casters to tell us to begin, just waiting for the battle to commence. My heartbeat starts to race, I'm flooded with adrenaline in anticipation of what's about to come next. I look over to Clarence, he looks back at me and nods, then we both look forward again.

"ARE, YOU, READY!?" one of the casters says and the crowd goes wild.

"Well then, what are we waiting for!?" The other exclaims.

"Three..." they say in unison, here we go, this is it. "Two...." I close my eyes for a brief moment and take a deep breath. "One..." I exhale and open my eyes ready for whatever comes next. "FIGHT!"

Clarence and I both immediately leap forward into a handspring, just as we practiced. As my hands touch the ground I look to see that both of our opponents are at a dead sprint away from us, apparently they have no intentions of hand to hand combat to start the fight either. Once I land I start running for the wall, Clarence does the same. I look and see that there are two long swords crossed and mounted on the wall strait away from us, perfect for Clarence. However, I see no spear, but I do see a shield roughly 20 feet away from the swords. It will have to do. Clarence and I

122

arrive at the wall at roughly the same time. I grab my shield and start to turn with it and I'm met by the sight of Clarence slicing an arrow in half not a foot from my face. I've been in battle for a minute tops and Clarence has already saved my life, some partner I am. "Thanks," I say.

"Anytime, now focus up!"

I look across the battlefield to see that the taller of the two is the archer, his shorter friend is wielding twin maces guarding his friend. Behind them I can see my spear hanging from the furthest wall, of course it would be on the side opposite us.

Clarence and I both start to run towards our opponents, blocking the volley of arrows the tall one is launching at us. As we close in on them the short one starts running to the right of us, and his partner strafes left. They must be trying to get us to pick a target so the other can come after us, either that or they want us to split up. "I GOT MACE, YOU GET BOW," Clarence shouts as he changes is trajectory. Without hesitating I start making my way closer to the archer, strafing diagonally at the same time so that I can cover Clarence's back.

I start to close the gap slowly, he's quite fast for someone who is shooting arrows, but I'm faster. I hear a clash of steel behind me, Clarence must have engaged the other one, but I can't afford to lose focus and see how he's doing. I finally manage to get close enough to the archer to make an attempt at an assault. He fires one last arrow at me, this time I don't block it. Instead I dodge left as I bring my shield back to strike him with it. I feel the corner of the arrow graze the middle of my neck as it passes. It stings, but it doesn't faze me. I leap into the air with my shield fully cocked intending to strike him with it as he reloads. As I come down bringing my attack forward he grabs his bow on opposite ends with both hands to block. My shield meets his bow and he slides his bow to the side with perfect timing in order to deflect the force that my shield is carrying. Without even thinking as my failed assault brings my shield crashing into the ground I counter by bringing my foot around towards his head, he counters again with his bow. This time twisting his bow around my leg and then spinning it, flipping me over and leaving me exposed. In the blink of an eye he draws an arrow and without knocking it in his bow he brings it down towards my leg with his hand. I slide my leg to the side causing him to strike nothing but the ground. I Trap his exposed arm between my legs now and roll opposite his body while dropping my shield and grabbing his hand with both of mine. This brings him crashing to the ground with me. I have him trapped in an armbar and pull with all of my might. I hear the terrible sound of his elbow snapping as I dislocate it and tear everything that was once whole inside. He screams in pain, but wastes no time reacting and before I can release him he drops the bow from his opposite hand in order to grab an arrow which he drives into my right calf. The pain is immense, but it won't stop me. Before he can withdraw from the assault on my leg I release his arm and lean forward to grab his other hand. He releases the arrow trying to escape, but it's no use. I slide my legs away from his body and then pull with all of my might on his only functional arm, causing him to land on his stomach. I spring to my feet, with his hand still secured and press my still impaled leg into his scapula with all of my weight while jerking his arm up and back with as much force as I can muster. Again I am met by the sound of his body tearing, only this time it's his shoulder. He screams in agony, one side of his body broken at the elbow, and the other at the shoulder. He's done and he knows it. I'm not leaving anything to chance though. I grab his already disfigured arm which I previously ruined, and do the same to it. I figure he will have a hard time doing much of anything with two dislocated shoulders.

Once this is done, I grab his remaining arrows from his quiver, as well as his bow, and toss them away. He just lays there sobbing, we both know it's over. I walk to my shield, which is laying on the ground a few feet away and pick it up. "Please…" he says between sobs, "please no." He starts to try and move himself away from me by dragging his feet in the sand. It's no use. I walk back to him and put my right foot in the center of his back, pinning him in place. "PLEASE!" I grab my shield with both hands, one on each side, and raise it above my head. "PLEASE I'M BEG-" His words are cut short as I drive the shield down into the base of his skull. His body goes completely limp. He is silent. It's over.

It's at this moment that I remember Clarence is fighting the other combatant. I turn and look across the arena to see the two still engaged. Clarence is on the offensive, but his opponent is blocking every attack. I need to help him. I look and see that the spear I had sought earlier wasn't far from where I was standing, so I start to run towards it, watching the battle as I do my best to get to my weapon. Clarence appears to have the upper hand, but no matter what he does he can't seem to connect with any of his attacks. I reach the spear and grab it from the rack. There is no time to waste, Clarence and the attacker are engaged at an angle so that only Clarence can see me. I turn towards them and take a deep breath to steady myself as I draw the spear above my shoulder. I take aim and muster all of the energy I have remaining to take a few steps forward and launch my spear at Clarence and the enemy. Clarence see's the spear flying through the air and takes a step to his right in order to cause his foe to counter by centering his back to the spear. Moments later the spear connects, piercing through our opponent's lower back on his right side. He stumbles forward, both caught off guard and in shock from the spear that is now piercing his body, with the front of it sticking out right above his right hip. Clarence wastes no time as he brings his swords down on either side of his opponent's neck causing his head to leave his body. Blood sprays from his neck and splashes across Clarence's chest and face as he falls to the ground lifeless. Now it really is over.

I look at Clarence, and he looks at me. His face the most stern and serious I have ever seen it, with his brow wrinkled and fierce eyes. He nods at me, and I nod back. It's then that I zone out and am met by the roar of the crowd. They are going ballistic. "WHAT A FINISH!" Blake shouts over the intercom.

"THERE YOU HAVE IT FOLKS, YOUR VICTORS! CLARENCE AND ROYCE!" Charles yells. I look back at Clarence to see him throwing his arms in the air celebrating to the crowd. I do the same. We both rotate around gesturing towards the roaring crowd before we finally drop our arms and make our way towards one another. We meet and high five as we go in for a pat on the back. We did it.

"That's my boy!" Clarence yells at me. "You do know you have an arrow sticking out of your leg though right?"

"I had totally forgotten about that..." I say as my sudden realization brings with it the pain of the injury. I groan and grimace from the pain. Clarence laughs at me. "Do I pull it out or leave it in?"

"I'd leave it in and let a doctor pull it out if I were you. Don't wanna do any more damage than is already done. Nice work though with that spear, I woulda had him, but you saved me some time and effort I guess."

"Yeah sure, you're welcome. Now can we go find a doctor?" Not a moment after the words leave my mouth a door starts to open on the edge of the arena, off to the left of where we came in about half way down. We start to walk towards it, and I'm met by more pain. "OW!"

"Come here you big baby," Clarence says as he puts my right arm around his neck and puts his left arm across my back to help me limp across.

"You know I could do it myself, I'm just letting you help me so the crowd can see how good of a team we really are."

"Tell yourself whatever you need to if it helps keep your ego afloat man."

"That's my story and I'm sticking too it." The pain grows as we make our way across the arena and my adrenaline fades. As we near the door I look back over my shoulder and see the bodies of our opponents laying on the ground. My heart sinks a little, but the smile on my face remains, more hollow now. I'm not sure what hurts worse, my leg, or knowing that we had to take two lives only moments ago in order to keep our own. It's a sickening feeling, especially since we will have to do it 19 more times in order to earn our freedom, or die trying. We will have to carry the weight of the two lives that we just took, as well as 38 more souls in the future should we continue to win.

It also sickens me to think about how easy it was to do it all. In the heat of the moment I didn't even think about what I was doing or the consequences of my actions, I just got caught up in the moment and acted accordingly, without hesitation. Clarence's opponent at least had a relatively quick death, mine met his end slowly. He had to endure immense pain and begged for his life before I finally ended it. My heart hurts just thinking about it. I wonder if other gladiators feel this way as well. Does Clarence feel this way? Part of me hopes he does, however part of me hopes he doesn't, I'd hate for him to be torn up inside the way I am. I feel as though I live in my head more than he or any of my friends do, so maybe it doesn't affect them as much. Maybe the 18 years of training and preparation for this makes them numb to taking a life. I wish I could be that way, I just overthink everything. I could never ask if they feel the same though. I don't want to show any signs of weakness. I'll carry this soul crushing weight with me to the grave.

IX

Clarence and I finally make it through the doors and are met
by four men, two of which are orderlies, and the other two are men

wearing all white with latex gloves. "Clarence you'll be coming with us to wait in the victors' lounge," One of the orderlies says. "Royce you'll be taken to the med bay with these two gentlemen to get patched up." That must mean that the two men in white are doctors or medical practitioners of some sort.

Clarence and I say our goodbyes, and just like that Clarence is gone. Now it's just me, and two men wearing all white who I can only assume are going to fix me up somehow. I'm just wondering how long I'm going to be out for, and if this will have any lasting effects or affect our training at all. Hopefully it doesn't set me back too much.

The hall that I am being wheeled down is just more cement. You would think that since this is the winning side there would be more decoration, a little more effort put into it so you at least feel like you won. Instead there is just more of the same, nothing is different. The two men don't talk, neither do I.

We come to a double door entry. The doors are all white with a window in the upper center of each door and metal framing. There is a keypad to the right of the doors, one of the men punches in a few numbers and suddenly the doors slide open, I wasn't even aware they were sliding doors. They push me through the entrance and into a room that I can tell is humungous by a long path ahead and tall ceilings, but is closed off by curtains everywhere. On either side of the path ahead there is great lengths of curtain, with occasional breaks that open up new paths. We move forward. As they push me I hear a faint whirring of machines everywhere. I look to the ground and see yellow lines painted on both sides of the path directly under the curtains that hang only a few inches from the ground and stand at least seven or eight feet tall. The curtains are a strange teal/aquamarine color that I wouldn't use if I was decorating the place, but it's nicer than cement I guess. I notice that occasionally there are numbers on the ground as well. All three digits long and seemingly sequential. We pass 001, 002, 003, and so on. Maybe the curtains are rooms? Maybe beds? I'm sure I'll find out soon enough.

We cover a decent distance before we finally stop by number 017. One of the men walks forward and pulls the curtain on the left to the side, revealing a small room that has nothing but a weird bed with a glass case over the top. It has a solid beige metal base and it is emitting the whirring sound I heard upon entering this monstrous area. The other man in white pushes me into the room. He then stops us, engages what I'm assuming are the brakes on the chair, lets go of it, and walks over the bed and presses a button near the head of it. Not a moment later the glass starts into the bed, disappearing completely and opening the bed. "Would you like any assistance?" He asks looking at me.

"Uhm, am I supposed to get in?" I respond. I'm not sure how this is supposed to work, but I feel weird about getting into a bed that makes machine noises and has a glass case that opens and closes around it.

"That's correct sir, would you like assistance?"

"I think I can manage." I place my feet on the ground and do my best to lift myself up by using mostly upper body strength and not my right leg, which still has the arrow in it. I wince in pain as I put some pressure on it, but then hop on my left leg over to the bed. I turn and sit on the bed. I take care when lying down so as not to bump the arrow at all.

The bed isn't comfortable at all, it seems to just be a glass base which I lay on with a small plastic mold to rest my head on for neck support. I look over and see the man who opened the bed push another button. This time a syringe pops out with a needle in it, as well as a wet cloth. He takes the cloth and moves down to my calf. He wipes the area above the arrow with the cloth that popped out for a few seconds and then grabs the syringe. "Slight pinch," he says as he buries the needle in my leg. I barely feel it, the arrow is a lot worse than a small needle.

Within seconds of the needle going into my leg I start to relax and the pain starts to fade. I'm not sure what he just did to me, but I'm perfectly okay with it. It feels as though a boulder was just removed from my chest and I can finally breathe easy again without any pain in my leg. I hear a strange squishing tearing noise near my leg and look down to see the man who injected me handing the arrow to the other man who then turns and walks out of the room. Did he really just rip an arrow out of my leg without me feeling a thing? Whatever he gave me really is amazing. "Put this on and breathe as though you normally would," he starts to say as he hands places a strange rounded triangular piece of rubber with a tube attached to it over my mouth and nose. "Lay back and relax now, and do your best to refrain from moving. The process is going to take roughly 15 minutes and should be relatively painless, but may cause slight discomfort. I'm strapping in your waist to make the process as easy and quick as possible." As he says this he pulls a polyester belt from the bed on either side of my body and hooks them together just above my waist. I'm not entirely sure what's about to happen, but I figure it can't be that bad after how easy getting the arrow out was. "Nod if you understand." I nod.

After I nod he steps back and presses another button, this time the glass comes back and encases the bed. He then turns and walks out of the room. I'm trapped now, but hopefully it's for the best. The bed starts to whir louder than before, I hear running water. My back gets wet, as well as the rest of my body that's touching the surface of the bed. The water starts to rise. I'm panicking a little as the bed starts to fill with water, but I try to stay relaxed like the man said. Before long I am completely submersed in water, the bed is completely filled inside the glass. It feels strange breathing through the strange rubber triangle on my face, but I see why he gave it to me. Suddenly the bed lights up near my head, and the light slowly travels down the bed to my feet, and then back up towards my head again before disappearing.

I hear a strange noise near my ear and can't help but look to my right. A small hole has opened in the top corner of the bed. A few moments pass and I see five tiny metal balls no larger than a grain of rice come out with four tentacles on each. They move themselves forward by spinning in a circle and using their tentacles to form a propeller and make their way towards my calf. I wonder what they are going to do. Upon reaching my calf they all stop spinning and touch down on my leg using their tentacles as legs now. They all circle my wound and I see a red fan of light emitting from one of them go up and down around the hole in my leg. The light goes away, and then without pause all five of the tiny metal balls go inside my leg one by one. This is starting to freak me out a little. Why are there metal balls with tentacles inside my leg? What are they doing? Should I be worried? I know the man said not to worry, but still it's a little concerning seeing little robot things climb inside my body.

I start to feel a strange tingle from the wound. It was numb before, but now that those things are inside me I have a strange sensation. I see my skin glowing around the wound, there is some sort of light being generated inside my leg. The tingling sensation starts to grow to a mild burn. Considering how numb I was before I find it surprising that I can feel anything at all at the moment. I lay and wait, watching my leg to see what will happen next.

The light remains constant, the burn stays mild and doesn't grow any more severe. Time passes and eventually one of the robots emerges, followed by another. They stand on either side of my wound and reach across with two tentacles each and pull the torn skin closer together slowly, closer and closer as more time passes. Finally another one emerges, then another shortly after, and then finally the last of the five. Once they are out the two that are pulling the skin together pull it to the point that the two sides are touching each other and the other three shoot a focused red beam of light at the now line that is my wound. The three of them move their beams very slowly in unison across the line from top to bottom, and as the beams move I see the red bleeding line slowing changing to a light pink line that is seemingly healthy skin. Once they have completely traversed the wound with their beams they stop, the beams go away, the two that are securing the skin release their grasp, and then the five of them float up in the water and start spinning towards the hole they came out of. Once they reach it, they enter it and the hole closes behind them, as though they were never here.

A few moments after the hole closes, I hear what sounds like a drain open up, and the water level starts to fall. Soon the water is completely gone, and the only evidence that it was ever there is my wet body. I hear a different whirring noise start, louder and more aggressive than the one before, and I start to feel warm air flow. I notice now that there are pores in the surface that I'm lying on and warm air is being emitted from them at a high speed. My body is being air dried. After a minute or two the air flow stops and the noise subsides. Now it's as if the water was never there.

I look to see the man who set everything up coming back in the room now. He walks up and presses a button, yet again, and the glass slides open. He then reaches over and undoes the polyester belt that was holding me in place. "Good as new," he says.

"What do you mean good as new?" I ask as I sit up in the bed.

"Your leg is all healed, it's as if it never happened. Granted you will have a slight pink tint where it was sealed up for a couple weeks, but that will fade in time. A month from now it will be as if it never happened."

"So I'm just good now? Nothing wrong? No wound? No need to worry about my training being affected or having to put off my next fight?"

"Yes sir, you're good to go. You could go back out there and do another fight right now if you had to and your leg wouldn't cause you any problems. Minor injuries like this are a pretty easy fix, there was no bone, joint, or nerve damage, just soft tissues that are easily repaired. Now if you're ready, I'll escort you to the victors' lounge and you can join your friend."

"Uh, alright then. I guess." I hop off the bed and I'm in disbelief. My leg feels totally fine, it really is as though nothing ever

133

happened. Nothing remains of the hole that was once in my leg except for a small pink line that isn't even noticeable if you aren't looking for it. This is amazing.

"Right this way sir." The man says as he turns and starts to walk out. I follow, the other man standing at the entrance to the room holding the curtain for us as we walk by. I'm led back the way we came to the double white doors, he puts in the code again and the doors open. We walk through the door and I'm free from the med bay. Hopefully I never have to come back here, but I feel like the odds of that are slim. I'll at least hope that I don't make this a regular thing.

We pass more and more cement, it makes me wonder how all the men working here know how to get around when everything looks basically the same. Soon we come to a door that leads us to a stairwell which goes up so many flights I don't even bother trying to count. Of course the stairs are cement too. The impressive thing about all of this is that my leg feels perfectly fine through all this walking, whatever that machine was it worked magic. We walk out and there is a short dimly lit hallway leading to a door. This time there is just one door though, it's solid black with a gray metal handle. An orderly is standing next to it, he doesn't even look at us. "Here you are sir, the victors' lounge. Inside you will find plenty of food and drink, as well as all of the other victors for the day, both male and female. You will remain here until all matches for the day have concluded at which point you will be escorted off the premises. Enjoy." Without pause the man in white turns and starts to walk away, leaving me outside the black door alone with the orderly who seems to be ignoring my existence.

I reach for the door and pause a moment once my hand touches the handle. The man in white said that there would be every victor on the other side of this door, from both sexes. That means that Dime will either be in there, or she won't. I know Gordon is in there, I know Clarence is in there, but in the heat of everything that had been happening the past short while I had totally forgotten about

Dime. She has to be in there. I'm pretty sure she will be, she's too good to fail in the first round. I hope she's in there. *Please be in there.*

I take a deep breath and turn the handle, opening the door. The inside looks almost exactly the same as the room we were in before the fights, the matted flooring, the table of all the food, the giant screen with the fights, the black couches, everything is more or less the same, with one key difference. On the far side of the room there isn't a wall, instead there is a giant glass window that overlooks the arena. Another key difference is that there are far less people inside since there haven't been too many fights yet. I look at the handful of faces in the room, Clarence and Gordon are sitting on the right side of the window, both of them have smiles on their face when they see me, there are a few others around them that must have been from the couple of fights that must've happened after ours, and on the far left side of the room in the corner of the window sits a long dark brown haired girl looking out the window. I can feel a smile grow across my face, and it's not because I see two of my best friends. It's because of her. Not only do I get the satisfaction of knowing she's okay, but I get to be in the same room with her again, nothing to keep us apart. My heart starts to race just from the sight of her. I step through the door and hear it close behind me as I start to make my way across the room towards her. She still hasn't noticed I'm here, too busy looking out over the arena. Before I even make it half way there my journey comes to a pause as Clarence grabs my shoulder. "MY MAN!" He says. "Look at you! You're walking just fine like nothing ever happened. What did they give you? Some sort of miracle juice to fix you up?" Dime looks our way from the commotion and I see a smile grow across her face, but its only for a moment before she turns back to the window.

"Something like that," I say with a half-smile.

"Well you can hardly tell that you were dumb enough to get stabbed by a guy with a broken elbow," Gordon chimes in. "So you've got that going for you, which is nice. I know if I were that stupid I would want them to cover up the evidence as soon as possible, wouldn't want your lady friend over there knowing how much of a loser you almost were." Even after getting pummeled to the point where I can see he's covered in bruises, there's still never a dull moment with Gordon. Or a moment of silence for that matter.

"Hey man don't listen to this guy," Clarence says, "a win's a win and it doesn't matter what happens as long as you get it. You would think Gordon would know that after his sorry showing."

"Hey all I'm saying is I currently hold the record for quickest match all season," Gordon says.

"Only because there's only been a handful of matches," I say. "And it was our first match, now I know to look out for that next time I'm snapping someone's arm. There's bound to be hiccups, learning curve and all that."

"You're getting caught up in the details," Gordon responds. "I've got the quickest match of the day, the season, and heck maybe the whole year."

"Not sure I'd be proud of that," Clarence says. "You probably lost half your earnings for that sorry display."

"Hey man, if I have to be a scumbag 40 times to get my freedom, that's fine. So long as I get it. I'd rather win the cheap way than lose the fair and square way."

"How did you come up with that strategy anyways?" I ask.

"Pretty simple really, I just went and asked around the training facility and found out who all of the diamond level fighters were, and then I did research on their strengths and weaknesses. I just had to have a strategy for every possible person I might be going up against, and that particular strategy was one I had in place for him and a few others. Guy sucks at hand to hand combat if you can get behind him, he has no shoulder mobility. Didn't you guys try to do any research?"

"I mean…" Clarence starts, "not really no. We just kind of prepared for whatever, figured there were too many people to try and study up on."

"And that's why I'll earn my freedom, and you'll get screwed at some point. Always do your homework boys, and then all you have to do is be willing to be viewed as a cheap piece of trash that no one wants to win for the remainder of your time as a gladiator. It's easy really."

"Only you could look at it that way Gordon," I say.

"Yeah man, what happens when your crazy strategies don't work?"

"They always will, that's the point. I don't care what it takes, I'm in it to win it, and I'll make it happen one way or another. If I have to kick dirt in your eyes, or spit on you, or even pull your drawers down, I'll do it. So long as I get that win. One down, 39 to go."

"That just seems like a whole lot of extra effort to me," I say. "I'd rather just train hard and be the stronger fighter, rather than rely on cheap tricks to get me through things."

"Yeah man, not to mention once people see you doing this regularly they are going to prepare for your cheap antics just in case they wind up facing you. I don't know man, just seems risky."

"How about you do things your way, even if it's not as good, and I'll keep doing things my way. Sound good? Good. Now if you'll excuse me, I have to go flirt with Kayleah before Royce can. I could tell by the way she was snarling at me earlier that there might really be something there, I just have to be willing to dig for it."

"You're going to have to dig way deep then man, because she ain't got no love for you, only love for my boy over here," Clarence says as he pats me on the back and shakes me a bit.

"Yeah please don't do that," I say. "Actually if you could just not even look at her, that would be great. I don't want her getting creeped out by you and then subsequently avoiding me by association. Go flirt with one of the girls at the food table from the doubles match. Maybe they're into cheapskates."

"ROYCE HOW COULD YOU SAY SOMETHING SO FOUL ABOUT SOMEONE AS NICE AS KAYLEAH!? FOR SHAME!" Gordon shouts at the top of his lungs. I hate him. I hate him so much sometimes. So much. "Good luck buddy, if you need me I'll be laying the moves on the two over there, maybe if you're lucky I'll share." I look over and Kayleah is looking at me with a perplexed look on her face. I really hope Gordon chokes on whatever food he is about to eat while talking to those girls.

"Good going Gordon," Clarence says as he smacks Gordon on the back of the head. They both walk over towards the food. "Go get her man," he whispers as he walks by.

Well this is it, no turning back now. I have to go talk to her after that, otherwise she will think I really was saying something bad about her and then she'll never talk to me again. Gordon has a way of making life more difficult than it needs to be at times. This is one of those times. I smile and wave at her like an idiot. She smiles and nods for me to come over before turning back towards the window. Maybe this won't be so bad after all. I slowly walk towards the couch she's sitting on, the couch being the only silver lining to this situation so I can sit next to her. I get to the couch, walk up next to her and sit down. I find myself at a momentary loss for words, I really should plan out what I'm going to say before I try to talk to her."H-hey," I say. Smooth.

"Hi," She responds as she looks me in the eye and greets me with a warm smile.

"Mind if I sit here?"

"Why do you think I decided to sit on a couch and not in a chair?"

"So you were expecting me then?"

"You could say that. Now that we've cleared that up, you have to tell me what the deal is with your friend over there. We've only talked twice, and he's been there both times to set you up for failure."

"Oh… you mean Gordon. Yeah…he's…different."

"I'm guessing you didn't say anything bad about me?"

"Of course not! He just likes to get a rise out of people. Sometimes I wonder why we keep him around, especially in situations like that."

"Well I'm sure it was all just in good fun."

"I mean yeah, he can get carried away sometimes, but usually he doesn't actually want to hurt anyone. He just thinks he's funny or something."

"You know he's different when you're not around right?"

"What do you mean?"

"Well him and I were the only two in here for a while since we were the first two fights. He just kept to himself, he basically grabbed some food and sat on the opposite side of the room from me. I wasn't sure if I should try to talk to him or not since he didn't seem to be giving off a very inviting vibe, so I just came over here and sat down."

"That doesn't sound at all like the Gordon I know. I figured he would have been pestering you until Clarence showed up and stopped him or something like that." It's strange for me to think of Gordon acting shy or sulking away from people in any setting. Maybe he doesn't act the same when he doesn't have any friends around? The thought never crossed my mind.

"Yeah he seems very peculiar that one. You'll have to formally introduce us at some point."

"I don't know about that, maybe way down the road after we've been talking for a few years and everyone is on the outside. Maybe then you can meet him. I don't want to scare you off after you hear some of the things that come out of his mouth. You might start to wonder why I associate myself with him and draw your own conclusions."

"I don't know about that, I think I know you pretty well on some levels. Well enough to not be scared off too easily." Hearing her say that makes my heart warm and a smile grow on my face.

"I'm glad you feel that way."

"Oh my gosh! I almost forgot, how is your leg!?" She looks down at my calf.

"It's actually surprisingly good."

"I saw you get stabbed though!"

"Yeah they put me in some sort of weird water tank medicine bed thing that fixed me up like nothing ever happened."

"Water tank medicine bed thing huh? Is that the official name for it?"

"It's a working title, I'm sure they'll change it eventually." I nervously laugh and scratch the back of my head.

"Well I'm glad that you're okay, my heart skipped a beat when I saw it happen."

"Yeah I felt pretty stupid in that moment, kind of embarrassing that you saw that."

"Hey it's your first fight, everyone makes mistakes."

"If that's the case how did your fight go? I didn't get to see it because we had to sit in the waiting room for the whole thing."

"It went good."

"It went good? That's it? Just good?"

"Yeah more or less, I mean she was decently formidable and managed to challenge me a little, but I never felt like she had the upper hand. I felt in control the entire time."

"What happened to 'everyone makes mistakes'?"

"Yeah… everyone but me maybe?" She lets out an awkward laugh.

"I don't think you can say everyone if you're excluding yourself."

"Okay, almost everyone makes mistakes then." She grins.

"I mean, I've seen you make your fair share of mistakes over the years."

"That's different though. That's part of the learning process. Ideally by now we've learned all we need to, and it's just about the application of what we've learned. Which is what I did. And I'm pretty sure I've seen you make a few more mistakes than me in class."

"That's because I was always too busy trying to stare at you." I smile intensely at her, she blushes slightly.

"Well look where that got you, an arrow in the leg."

"I'd say it was worth it if it meant I got to see you even a little bit more than I would have otherwise."

"Is that so? So you're saying you don't mind being stabbed in the leg so long as you get to see me?"

"I mean I wouldn't put it like that, but I would say that I value seeing you and am willing to sacrifice to do so."

"I like that," she says softly, her voice barely above a whisper. "Just don't sacrifice too much okay? You need to stay focused and win or you won't get to see me. This time it was an arrow to the leg, next time could be worse. Take care of yourself."

"Hey I'm not planning on going anywhere. One fight down and nineteen to go. You don't distract me, you motivate me. Especially now that I know we will get to see each other after we win if we can fight on the same days. I have no intentions of dying on you."

"Promise?"

"I promise I'll make it so long as you do."

"Good, me too." She grabs my hand and leans her head onto my shoulder. I can feel her smiling with her head leaned on me even though I can't see her face. There's no way I'm not going undefeated now. I don't care who they put Clarence and I up against. I'll take as many lives as I have to just to be able to see her after every match. Maybe that's why they let us mingle with the victors of the opposite sex after each fight, just that much more motivation. Well it's working, and I don't care. It's odd to think about how we are just sitting here together, her body nestled up against mine, totally relaxed, as we overlook thousands of people and watch other gladiators fight to the death. Some romantic scene this is. It doesn't even matter though, regardless of our surroundings, just having her here with me makes me happy, makes me complete, makes me want more and more for the rest of forever. I'll fight for this with everything I have for as long as I can just for this moment, this connection, this feeling right here.

"Kayleah..."

"Yeah?" she says softly.

"I know we've only spoken to each other twice, but we've known one another on some level for years. There's something that is tearing me up inside, trying to find its way to my lips in the form of words like it's going to explode out of me if I don't say it, so I'm just going to do it. I think I'm falling in love with you." A few moments of silence form. She grabs my hand even tighter.

"Well I guess you'll just have to keep winning to see if you fall all the way or not." I can feel her smile against my shoulder. I'm taking that as her saying she might be falling for me too, and I don't know that my heart could be any fuller than it is right now. A large part of me wants to try and kiss her, but there are orderlies in the room and I don't know if that's allowed. Better to play it safe and keep the good feeling going than to risk ruining it and being carted off. "Maybe if you're lucky and you play your cards right, I might just fall for you too." *Screw it.* As soon as the words leave her mouth without hesitation I grab her chin with my opposite hand and lift it as I go in for a kiss. Time stands still as our lips meet for the second time ever. This kiss just as good as the last, maybe even better. I feel her leave mine as she wraps one arm around the back of my head and the other around my back. We become one. The touch of her soft lips envelops me along with her intoxicating scent as I take a deep breath trough my nostrils drawing in her essence. The warmth of her body against mine, the tingling of her hair brushing against my skin, everything is right in the world in this moment. Within moments, however, it comes to a crashing halt as I feel a hand on each shoulder and an arm under each armpit as two orderlies drag me away from my perfect moment. I see her smile as I'm carted off.

"No kissing allowed," one of them says as they tote me to the far side of the room. "First offense gets you stuck on the opposite side of the room, try to go near her again and you'll spend time in the box." It was worth it. Especially because now I know I get to see her after every match so long as we both win every time. The orderlies release me in the opposite corner near a couch facing towards her, so I decide to just stay there. "You've been warned."

I look and see Kayleah staring at me, but only for a moment. As soon as our eyes meet she smiles and turns back towards the window, just as she was when I first walked in. I look over and see Gordon and Clarence talking to the two girls they had walked over towards earlier, they both looked over at me and smiled and nodded. Gordon then flexes at the girl he's talking to and struts a little bit. He knows no shame, he also probably has no idea what he's doing. To be fair though, none of us do. Clarence appears to just be playing it cool like he always does. It makes me happy knowing that everyone that I needed to win today did just that, regardless of how it happened. For at least a little while longer the crew is still whole. Now all we need is for Joseph to pull through on his match this week and we will be set. For now though, I'll just sit and watch my friends as they entertain themselves, as well as others. Maybe if I'm lucky I'll catch the occasional glance from Kayleah and feel the rush of our eyes meeting yet again. I may have been stabbed in the leg today, and had to take two lives today, but even after all of that I must say. Today is a good day, even if it isn't even half over yet.

I watch Gordon and Clarence talk with their respective girls for quite some time. I can tell Gordon isn't making any ground with his, because she just looks uncomfortable. That doesn't stop him from relentlessly trying though. Clarence's girl seems to be impressed however, they are just standing next to one another conversing with smiles on their faces. Kayleah is still in her corner, just staring out over the crowd and battles. As time passes, victors trickle in little by little. After a while there is a decent amount of people present, we must be at least half way through the day's matches. I could probably find out if I cared to watch the show and listen to what the commentators have to say, but I'd rather watch my friends and see what they're doing. I've seen my share of death today anyhow.

I hear the door open and shut every time new victors enter the room, so it catches my attention when I hear it open, and a brief pause follows. The door hasn't shut. I turn to look towards the door, as does everyone else in the room. All conversing amongst us comes to a halt as we stare at a man standing in the doorway holding it open, staring back at us. A man in his early 30s wearing a black suit with a light blue dress shirt and black tie holding a briefcase. His hair is nothing more than dark stubble. He has strong cheek bones and ridges running up either side of his forehead. The thing that really stands out about him though, is his piercing light blue eyes that sit below his focused, wrinkled brow. After he scours the crowd for a moment, his gaze finds its way to me and we lock eyes. I see a slight smile appear in the corner of his mouth. Is he looking for me?

The man finally steps into the room, letting the door close behind him, and makes his way towards me. I look around to see if there is any chance he is walking towards anyone that isn't me, but I'm the only one sitting here. He stops just a few feet in front of me. "Hello, it's Royce right?" His voice is soft and calm, but firm, just a few steps above a whisper.

"Yes, that's me." What does this man want with me? Did I do something wrong? Is this about me kissing Kayleah?

"Please allow me to introduce myself, my name is Micah, and if it's alright with you, I'd love a few moments of your time." His voice is oddly soothing, between the softness of it and his speech pattern. He annunciates everything with precision and slight pauses in his sentences.

"Yeah that's fine I guess, might I ask what it's regarding?"

"Your future." I'm curious now what he means when he says my future. "Now, if you don't mind, I'd appreciate it if you could go and, gather your friend Clarence as well. I'd love the opportunity to talk to, both of you."

"Uhm, alright I guess." I look towards Clarence, who is staring at us along with everyone else, and nod for him to come over. Clarence nods back and starts making his way towards us.

"What's up man?" Clarence says as he gets to us.

"This is Micah, and he wants to talk to us about our future I guess."

"That's correct," Micah says as he reaches out to shake hands with each of us. "As he said, my name is Micah, and I'd like to talk to the two of you about, your future. Now, I am what the business calls a, handler, and it is my job to essentially procure opportunities for, my clients, which is what I would like you two to be. You see, I like to think of myself as a, talent scout, and I see potential with you two. While most other handlers will wait until, week two or three of a season before engaging new potential clients, I like to start early. I look for certain, traits and talk to potential clients right away. I wouldn't want you two being taken off the market before we've had a chance to, talk."

"What exactly would you be 'handling' for us?" Clarence asks.

"Yeah, and how come we've never heard about handlers until now?" I add.

"Well, you see, handlers are strictly, behind the scenes. We simply orchestrate things for our, clients. When a gladiator starts to do well, and I believe you two will do very well, it starts to gather the, interest, of the public. It's my job to, capitalize, on that interest and, use it to our advantage. I will be doing things such as arranging private meetings with interested parties, acquiring sponsorships from various brand names, getting new equipment for the two of you through various channels, and ultimately doing my best to put you two in the best situation to have the crowd on your side. I will make you two a household name, everyone will be talking about you, and from that you'll be able to cash in. Now, you may not be able to leave the training facility or the arena on your own terms, but handlers, such as myself, have certain pulls and can acquire certain privileges for you to be able to step out into the real world, on occasion. And the best part is, I'll be depositing all of the money raised from these deals into accounts for you two to use once you earn your freedom. How does that sound?"

"Sounds pretty good to me!" Clarence says. "Sign me up!"

"What do you get out of all this?" I ask.

"Well, as you may have guessed, this does come at a price. The standard rate for handlers these days is forty percent of every deal I make for you. Naturally this does not affect the money you earn winning fights, but it does, however, affect just about all other earnings. Plus, should you two fail to achieve your freedom, and meet an unfortunate end, I shall receive all finances deposited for the two of you. This is all very standard. Just know that you won't find a better handler out there, and I'm going to be making us a lot of, money. So what do you say?"

"Can we have a moment to discuss it?" I ask.

"But of course, I'll wait over by the door, just signal me when you've decided." Micah turns and walks away.

"What're your thoughts man?" Clarence asks.

"Well the forty percent seems high, but he says he can get us better gear down the road. It also would be cool to be able to go out on occasion and see what the world is really like. Not to mention the extra money would be good for when we hit twenty wins, we wouldn't have to worry about having money once we earn our freedom. I just don't know if we should be agreeing to anything after just one match and talking with one guy."

"Well he did say that most of em are going to come at us in a couple weeks, he just likes to get the ball rolling early, and I like that. Plus I'm all about first come first serve, and since he came to us first, I'm more than willing to sign with him."

"I guess it doesn't really matter either way who we sign with, we still have nineteen matches to win regardless. Do you want to just do it and see what happens?"

"You already know I'm in, let's do it man. What have we got to lose?"

"Alright, screw it lets go." I don't know how I feel about this situation, it makes me a little uncomfortable agreeing to terms with a man we've only just met and trusting him without knowing if he's just telling us lies to get us to go with him or what. I guess we'll find out though.

I signal to Micah that we're ready and he walks back over to us. "So, what have we decided, gentlemen?"

"We'll do it," Clarence says.

"I'm glad to hear that, you've made a, good decision, and you won't be disappointed."

"I hope you're right," I say.

Micah pulls out his briefcase and sets it in front of us, he opens it and reveals a computer screen with words all across it and a pad with the outline of a hand on it. "This is my contract, it basically states that I will be working, for you, for forty percent of your earnings. It also states, that you will not be working with any other, handlers. It's all very standard, you can read through it, if you'd like. Once you're ready I just need you to place, your hand on the scanner. The scan will act as a, signature, and then we will be in business."

"Well I think you seem like a cool guy so I'm just going to sign," Clarence says as he puts his palm on the scanner.

"I was going to at least read it…" I say. "But you already signed for yourself so whatever I guess." After Clarence is scanned he removes his hand and I place mine on the scanner. When there's 19 opportunities for you to lose your life in the near future, signing a questionable contract with someone you've only just met really doesn't seem like a big deal. My scan finishes and I remove my hand, just like that we're in business with Micah for the foreseeable future.

"It's been a pleasure gentlemen, and I look forward to working with you," Micah says as he closes the briefcase and picks it up. "Now that we are in business, I plan to start right away. Once you are finished here today, they will, inform you on how to get new matches. You do so by pressing a button in your, room. The button signals you are prepared, and ready, for the next possible match. I suggest you do so tonight. If we want to get you two support, we need to start by putting you in the, spotlight, as soon as possible. If you two get on it tonight, and there's room at the very end of the week we may be in, luck. There's a chance you may be able to be one of the final fights of the week, which would have you fresh in everyone's memory moving, forward. Good luck gentlemen, you'll be hearing from me very, soon."

"Thanks," Clarence and I both say as Micah turns and starts to walk away.

"Well I don't know about you, but I'm gonna ready-up as soon as we get back to our room. No point in wasting time waiting forever between fights. The sooner we get our twenty the better anyways, right?" Clarence says.

"Yeah makes sense to me."

"Plus if we can play our cards right and he can set us up to earn some extra financial support for when we win our freedom, I'm even more on board."

"I guess we'll just have to wait and see." I'm uncertain about how I feel with regards to what just happened. Did we make the right decision? Is this going to benefit us moving forward? Regardless of what I think however, it doesn't change the fact that we just signed a contract and we're stuck with it now. Micah seems like a nice enough guy, and I like how he chose us out of all the other fighters on day one of the season, before all the fights have even happened too. I do know that regardless of what he does or doesn't do for us, we still have 19 more fights to win and nothing is going to change that.

"What did that stiff want?" I hear off to my left, of course Gordon would have to come give his input.

"That guy just signed us to a contract to make a bunch of cash, that's what he wanted," Clarence says with a big grin.

"Oh he was a handler huh?" Gordon says.

"How do you know about handlers?" I ask.

"How do you guys not know about handlers? It's as though you two idiots don't ask your instructors all the questions about everything you could possibly think of with regards to the arena…"

"Some of us were more focused on being ready for the fighting part…" I say.

"Well some of us are just good at fighting already and want to be well informed," He retorts with a smug look. Gordon is such an out of the box off the wall thinker all the time, he would have probably been successful in life if he had been his parents' first child and not the third. "Kind of weird how he came up to you two on day one though, my instructor told me that it's usually a few weeks in so they can see who really stands out. Maybe he just chose you because he felt sorry for you for being the only person in the history of the show to be stabbed by an arrow."

"Or maybe he just knows talent when he sees it," Clarence says. "I doubt you'll even get a handler with how you plan to play the game anyways."

"Meh, I don't really want one, or need one for that matter. I'm just here to do my piece and get out. I'll figure out the rest once I've earned my freedom. Plus, everyone will know my name before they know yours. 'Oh hey, did you guys hear about that guy that wins in the worst ways possible every time? Man I can't wait to see what crazy stunt he schemes up next!' I'll have all sorts of handlers lining up just to cash in on how underhanded I can be."

"You have to be the only person I've ever met that is actually looking forward to fighting dirty," I say.

"Yeah, but ya still love me!"

"Love is a strong word," Clarence says.

"But ya still like me!"

"Like is a strong word as well," I say.

"But ya still tolerate me!"

"For now," Clarence says. We all laugh. Gordon may be planning on fighting as unfair as possible to get to the top, but he's still our friend and we don't want to see him lose.

"Anyways, I should probably get back over there. This chick is acting like she doesn't have any interest at all in me, but I can tell that deep down she really wants me, I just have to keep at it." Gordon says.

"Good luck with that man," Clarence says as Gordon starts to walk away.

"Aren't you going to go talk to your girl?" I ask.

"Nah man, talking to girls is fun and all, but I don't want to get too attached to anything that might not be there when I get out in the end."

"Yeah I can't really say the same," I say with a half-smile as I scratch the back of my head. Clarence has the right idea, I just can't resist Kayleah. It's not necessarily a bad thing, it just might not be a good thing either.

"Hey man don't get me wrong, I think what you and Dime have is great. She seems to make you happy, and you two have had a

151

weird chemistry thing going on since day one before you even talked to her. You do you, I just don't have anyone like that, and I don't really want to find anyone like that and risk losing them. I have enough people to worry about between Gordon, Joseph, and yourself. Keep doing what you're doing man, I'm sure everything will work itself out in the end." I feel a little better hearing him say that, but deep down I know there's the chance that she doesn't make it and I'm devastated. Honestly if anyone close to me doesn't make it I don't know what I'll do. I'll have to find some way to manage and move on, I just don't know how. I guess that's future Royce's problem though; well hopefully it's not, but if something should happen it is I guess.

"Thanks man, I really appreciate it," I say.

"No problem, I'll always have your back. Whether it be physically on the field, or mentally off of it. I'm always here for you man, and I know you're here for me. It's been you and me since day one, and it'll be us 'til the end too man." Clarence's words are exactly how I've felt ever since I've known him. It feels good knowing he feels the same.

"You and me until the end," I say back. Clarence and I nod at each other and then decide to get some food and watch the fights. We decide to reward ourselves with fresh fruit and lean cuts of meat since we won our first match. Back on the super food as soon as we get back from the arena. The fights are always good to watch, most of them are close, and others are not. It's nice to see what the talent in our class is like. We pay extra close attention to the doubles matches because we may end up facing them down the road.

I shoot the occasional glance over in Dime's direction. I know I can't go over and talk to her again, but it's still nice to just look at her from time to time. It makes me happy. I never manage to catch her looking back at me though, but that's alright. I figure she must be stealing the occasional look whenever I'm not. I'll just have to win my next match to have the chance to spend time with her again, assuming they are on the same day. I will be pretty upset if our fights just never match up and we are always fighting on separate days, but we are both diamond so there's a pretty good chance that we fight around the same time most of the time. I'll just have to hope for the best I guess, which is what I feel like I always have to do considering everyone I care about has to fight for the life on a semi-regular basis now. Who knows, maybe we will both manage to actually earn our freedom some day and be able to start a real life together, that would be nice.

Daydreaming about an ideal future and watching fights consumes the rest of my time in the victors' lounge. Fights pass, winners enter, and eventually the room starts to feel rather crowded. The light outside starts to dim. As night approaches more and more people stare out the window instead of at the screen, none of us have ever seen a sunset before. None of us have ever seen the sun before either, or the sky, it's all new. Sadly, we can't actually see the sunset when it comes though, the walls of the arena are too high. We can however see the beautiful cascade of colors that stretches across the sky as the sun lowers out of our sight. What once was blue switches to orange, and then shades of red and purple start to leak through as the light fades and the darkness takes over. It then switches to total darkness, just a black night sky, with the only light being from the moon, which is also beautiful to see in person for the first time. It doesn't cast much light on us, only a sliver is visible, but it's beautiful none the less. The only saddening part about this whole experience is that there are no stars. The bright lights from the stadium drown them all out. All we can see is darkness, and the moon. Maybe someday if we are lucky enough to make it out of this we will be able to go outside on our own and be able to look up and see a sky full of white dots, rather than total darkness. Something to look forward to I guess, just one more thing to fight for. That's one more thing that motivates me, and I'm not sure if others are driven by it; I want to go out into the world and experience all the beauty it has to offer. I want to see, taste, and feel everything the world has to offer. I want to experience nature for the first time, and not just see pictures or look at it through the windows of the victors' lounge. I want to smell a flower, lay in the grass, eat a grape that is seconds removed from the vine that nurtured its development. There's so much more to life than what we have been able to see and do, and I want to experience all of it. I just have to earn it.

Eventually the final fight concludes, and the final victor joins us. After that there is a short lull before the door opens and an orderly is standing there waiting. "On behalf of everyone at the arena I would like to congratulate all of you on your hard fought victories today," he says. "From here I will escort you back to the train, which will take you back to the training center. Once there you will be free to carry on just as you did before today. From now on there will be a theater room open to everyone to go and watch the fights at any time of day, it is marked on your campus map in your rooms. You will also find that there is a button in a glass case on a stand next to the door in your rooms as well. This is the ready-up button. Press this when you are prepared for your next match and one will be assigned to you as soon as possible. You will be notified when the match will be within twenty-four hours of pressing the button. You will also notice there is a timer below the button, this is a countdown that starts at thirty days and counts down to zero, if you do not press the button for thirty days it will automatically activate and assign you a match. Now if you'll please follow me in an orderly fashion we will make our way to the train and prepare for departure. Thank you for your cooperation." The orderly turns and starts to walk away, and everyone trickles in behind him.

The first day of the season is officially coming to a close. One win down, nineteen to go. Five percent of the way there. I just have to stay confident, and keep training as hard as I can and I know we can do this. As soon as we get back to our room we will press that button, and then it's just a matter of repeating the process over and over until we have our freedom. There's a long road ahead of us, and I think today proves that we are ready to walk it.

X

Waking up the day after our fight is strange, not because I had nightmares about what had happened the day before, or even because I have a guilty conscience about what I did or even feel about it. It's weird, because I don't feel bad. We have been trained our entire lives to prepare ourselves to kill or be killed, so much so that I don't feel anything. I feel calm, cold even. There's no sadness, no regret, no fear or anger, there's nothing. It's as if there's a piece of me that should be there, but it isn't. Something's just… missing. It doesn't bother me in the sense that I'm freaking out because I don't feel anything, it bothers me because I feel as though I should. I wonder if Clarence feels the same way. Maybe everyone handles things like this differently, maybe I'm the same as everyone else, or maybe I'm just messed up. I try not to think about it, but I can't think of anything else. It's a strange concept to be stuck on, I'm not thinking about taking a life, or anything that I did the day before really, I'm just stuck on the fact that I'm empty right now.

I look at the clock, it's 5:55 am, five minutes until we start our day. I would get up now, but I don't know if Clarence is awake or not. When we got to our rooms last night we pressed the button. Now we just have to wait and see if we get a match or not. I'm honestly not even sure how it works, Do they tell us in person after the 24 hour window the orderly mentioned? Or do we get some sort of paper telling us? They don't really give us too much information on these things, but I guess it's not that important. It's not like it would change how Clarence and I go about our days for the rest of the week.

Thinking about it now, we didn't even know for sure if we would be fighting yesterday, we just assumed we would. I don't know if Joseph knew he wouldn't be fighting or if he just didn't ever get the knock at his door. I feel like that has to be nerve wracking if he doesn't know. Having to wake up every morning not knowing if today is the day you fight. I would want to know. I guess we'll see later if we run into him or not.

I hear the alarm start to go off and Clarence silences it almost immediately. He must have been awake for a while as well. We start to get ready for our day, Clarence seems normal enough. Maybe he isn't bothered by what we did either? I wonder if everyone is that way, I wonder if anyone else thinks about it as much as I do. Probably not.

We arrive at the weight room and make our way to the bench press and start warming up. About fifteen minutes into our workout we hear a familiar voice, "Man they really will let just about anyone in here won't they?" I hear Gordon say as he walks over alongside Joseph. I guess this means that Joseph isn't fighting today either.

"Apparently," Clarence says, "After all they did let you in here, and no one likes you, so that says something right there."

"They don't have to like me; they just have to respect me."

"I don't think they can even do that," I say.

"They don't have to respect me; they just have to put up with me."

"I don't know about that either," Clarence says.

"They don't have to put up with me; they just have to deal with the fact that I'm gonna be here for a while and there's nothing those losers can do about it! How about that!?"

"I mean yeah, that works I guess," Clarence says. Everyone laughs. It's nice having us all together again after three of us have had our fights. All Joseph has to do is pull through his and we will be guaranteed that much more time together. That is, depending on whether or not Clarence and I actually get a fight on Saturday.

"Congratulations by the way," Joseph says with a warm smile, "I'm glad you two were successful in your first match. Five percent of the way to freedom, it doesn't seem like much now, but inches make miles eventually." Leave it to Joseph to lift the atmosphere, hearing him say things like that with a smile always

156

warms my heart, no matter what the circumstances. I feel like I could get the worst news of my life and Joseph could cheer me up and take my mind of things for at least a little while. Out of all of us, I really think that Joseph is too good for this place. He deserves better.

"Thanks man," Clarence says, "You excited for your match?"

"I don't know if excited is the right word, more like anxious. I know once I get there I'll be fine, but the waiting and not knowing is what is killing me. I wake up every morning and wait for there to be a knock at my door, but so far there hasn't been one. I just hope I don't have to wait until Saturday, that would be the absolute worst!"

"I'm sure it will be soon," I say.

"Not like it matters," Gordon chimes in, "You're gonna win regardless. Thanks to my expert training that I've put you through over the years there's no way you can fail." Gordon poses with his fists on his hips and his chin held high as though he's just won an award.

"Yeah because you had anything to do with Joseph being the stud he is," Clarence says.

"I mean he's probably drastically improved Joseph's tolerance for ignorance and stupidity," I say.

"So what you're saying is," Gordon starts, "that thanks to me Joseph is a better person in multiple avenues and thus if he wins his fight I ultimately had something to do with it thanks to my contributions to his character development. I'm taking it as a compliment, thanks guys you're the best!"

"I mean that's not exactly where we were going with it," I say, "but hey whatever makes you feel better I guess."

"I'm sure it will all be fine," Joseph says, "I just have to keep training and be prepared for whenever the match may be. You've all helped me in your own way just by being there for me over the years, and I'm sure you'll all continue to do so for years to come should everything work out in our favor."

"I think that's what we're all hoping for," I say.

"How about this," Clarence says, "we meet here first thing in the morning the next few days. If Joseph doesn't show up, we know he's fighting and we can go watch. On Saturday if he hasn't fought yet we will know that has to be the day, and if Royce and I aren't fighting that day too, we can all go watch the fights to support him from here."

"That sounds like a great plan to me," Joseph says.

"Wait..." Gordon says, "Why would you two dinkuses be fighting on Saturday?"

"We pressed the button already, our handler told us it was a good idea to get more exposure and if they can't fill the ticket for Saturday we may have a chance to fight," I respond.

"What's a dinkus?" Clarence says.

"It's more or less you and Royce, you know... Idiots."

"Hey man," Clarence starts, "the way I see it, we have to win 20 fights and the sooner we can do that the better. No point in waiting around and dragging it out forever."

"I still think you should take some time to breathe, but that's just me. You know, the smartest guy in the group."

"I mean I hope that I don't have to wait until Saturday to fight," Joseph says, "but if I do I hope that the two of you can as well, that way we can see one another there."

"And that way Gordon can just listen to himself talk all day without any of us having to hear it," Clarence says.

"You say that I like to talk a lot, but I'm just sitting here listening to you spout off nonsense, so which of us really has the problem here?"

"I think we're getting a little off topic here guys," I interject.

"Sounds like a plan though," Joseph says, "we meet here every morning and if I can't make it you guys can watch the fights and be with me in spirit. If Saturday comes and I still haven't fought, I'll hopefully be able to see the two of you there to support me from the sidelines, and Gordon can still watch from here."

"I mean I don't know if I'll watch," Gordon says, "I've got a lot of stuff on the docket this week, and there's no point in watching a fight you already know the outcome of anyways."

"Man shut up," Clarence says, "you know you're gonna be there to support your boy."

"I guess we'll just have to wait and see now won't we?" Gordon says.

"We really should start our workout," Joseph says with a smile, "it was nice seeing you guys this morning. We'll see you tonight at dinner." He turns and looks at Gordon.

"Yeah he's right, feel free to look around while you two are lifting if you wanna see how real men get it done," Gordon says as he puffs up and turns to strut away.

"Whatever man," Clarence says.

"See you guys later," I add.

It's relieving to know that Joseph is here and isn't fighting right now, and it's also a relief that we have a plan in place to be able to watch Joseph's fight regardless of what happens the next few days. Even if he fights tomorrow, it won't kill us to take some time off of training to watch our friend fight. I'm sure he did the same for us.

Clarence and I fall back into our routine after that, we spend the rest of the day as we have just about every other day in recent weeks and train our hearts out. We push our limits as much as possible just doing our best to better ourselves in preparation for the next fight. It sucks not knowing when it will be, or who it will be against, so we just do our best to be our best for when the time comes.

That night we see Joseph and Gordon at dinner, and it's more or less the same as usual. The only difference being that all of us have the same thing in the back of our minds. We're all wondering if tomorrow will be the day. No one brings it up though. We just carry on as though everything is normal. Gordon makes bad jokes and draws attention to himself, Clarence and I try to put him in his place, and Joseph does his best to bring positivity and good vibes to the table. No one wants to address the elephant in the room, especially since we had already talked about it earlier that morning. Bringing it up again would just add to the anxiety and put tension in the air.

Sometimes I wish I could just skip ahead in life to the point where we get out of this place. But then again, I don't know that we will, and if skipping ahead means I skip to my death before leaving this place then I don't want to do that at all. The only thing worse than being in the position we are in is ceasing to exist in my opinion. While we may not be the happiest bunch at times, and our lives may be rough in some aspects, at least we do have lives to live. That's the only thing I can really thank the academy for is giving all of us a chance to live a life at all, rather than being aborted. It's terrible what they do, but ultimately it's the government that is forcing people to pay unreasonable fines or abort their children. I wish we could have all existed in a time before population was an issue. We may have never met, but at least we would all have the opportunity to live fulfilling lives and choose what we do with them. Wishing doesn't get anyone anywhere though, and day dreaming doesn't do anything for me in the end. I have to face up to reality and just suck it up and trudge down the rough road ahead. Either everything will work out, or it won't. Crying about it isn't going to change anything.

Maybe if we can all make it through this we can tell our story and see if we can't affect positive change some day.

That night when Clarence and I get back to our room there is an envelope on the floor just inside the room. We open it and read that we will be fighting on Saturday after all. Clarence acts excited at the news, I try my best to do the same, but I'm not looking forward to it.

I lay in bed staring at the ceiling before falling asleep. New fighters will be competing all week, Sunday through Saturday, and Joseph could be any day now. Today is only Monday and already I can tell Joseph is stressed about it. I'm relieved that Clarence and I already got ours out of the way and we know for certain we won't be fighting again until Saturday. I honestly hope that I don't see Joseph tomorrow. I hope that his time comes and he's able to go and lay it all out there and come back victorious. I don't like waiting to see if my friends are going to be here still next week any more than he likes waiting to see when he will have to fight. Only time will tell I guess.

Tuesday comes, Clarence and I wake up as usual, and go to the weight room first thing to see if Joseph will be there, and he is. We tell them we are fighting Saturday. Joseph congratulates us, Gordon mocks us. Basically what we expected. Wednesday comes and we do the same, and there he is again, you can see the anxiety is starting to wear on him. Thursday comes and goes the same as well. Finally Friday morning arrives and we head to the weight room, this time we are sure he won't be there, but shortly after we start our workout he shows up. He looks a little bit happier today than he has to past couple of days though.

We ask him what changed, and he explains that he is just relieved to finally know when he will be fighting. He's also happy that we will be there with him, that way he has a support system and he can be there for us as well. Always finding the silver lining. Joseph and Gordon leave to go do their own thing and Clarence and I get into our workout.

That night at dinner Clarence and I go to our usual spots after grabbing our delicious paste that we've grown so fond of, in the sense that we hate it but need it. Before long Joseph and Gordon join us.

"Well here we are again," I say. "Six days ago we were more or less in the same position, not knowing what tomorrow would bring."

"I mean at least I know it's for sure happening tomorrow," Joseph says.

"Yeah man the waiting game must've sucked," Clarence says.

"Oh yeah, I definitely don't recommend it. I mean it's nice that I've had this much more time to prepare, but I wouldn't have minded if they let me get it over with on Sunday like the rest of you."

"Well thankfully everyone but Gordon will be going tomorrow," I say.

"You say that like you're happy I'm not gonna be there," Gordon says.

"Well I mean it'll be easier on our ears," Clarence jabs.

"Hey, if anything I'm doing you a service. There's nothing your opponent can say to try and throw you off your game that I haven't said to you already, and I've probably said worse because I'm the best at everything I do."

"Well we've gotta give him that," I say, "he is the best at being the worst."

"You know, I'm gonna sleep like a baby tonight because I have nothing to worry about tomorrow, while the rest of you will be tossing and turning wondering what will happen. I'm actually looking forward to it, maybe I'll even sleep in a little."

"Do what you gotta do man," Clarence says.

We all banter back and forth for a while as we eat our dinners. One by one we finish, but no one wants to get up and leave. This time feels even harder than the last. It makes me wonder if the night before every fight is going to be even more difficult than the last. I don't want to have to do this 18 more times. I want to sit at this table with my friends for as long as possible and just pretend everything is going to be okay and nothing bad could possibly happen tomorrow, but it might. Everyone is going to do their best, and that's all we can do, and that just has to be enough.

Joseph is the last one to finish his meal, he sets down his fork on his tray and just looks at everyone with a heartwarming smile. "Well I guess this is it," he says, "I'll see everyone the day after tomorrow if I don't see you at the fights I guess. Wish me luck!" He grins from ear to ear and his eyes squint like they always do when he smiles.

"Good luck man," Clarence says.

"Good luck Joseph, I'm sure you'll do great and we'll be there with you every step of the way."

"Whatever, good luck I guess, not that you need it," Gordon adds.

Everyone gets up and prepares to leave. "Good luck to you guys too," Joseph says, "I'm sure you'll do great tomorrow."

"Thanks man," Clarence and I both say. We all turn and go our separate ways. Tomorrow is another big day, both for us and for Joseph. I don't know how I feel about us fighting tomorrow. Part of me wants to go and get it over with, but part of me also wants to be able to sit and watch Joseph and not have to worry about our fight. Oh well, it's out of my hands what happens at this point.

Clarence and I get back to our room and get ready for bed as usual. We both climb into our respective beds and turn off the light.

We don't say anything, because there's nothing to be said. We know what tomorrow brings.

The following morning eyes open and I am calm. There is no emotion running through me in this moment. I lay in bed and stare up at the ceiling for a moment before looking over to check the time, it's 5am. I have an hour before we have to start our day. I could go back to sleep, and in these situations I usually would, but I'm not tired. I feel calm and free of desire and emotion. I'm not sleepy, not hungry, not tired, not anxious or mad or happy or anything, I just am. This feels as though it is the true calm before the storm. I am as relaxed as I can be just laying in bed, with nothing to do for an hour. An hour with nothing but my thoughts to keep me company. An hour of silence.

I lay in bed staring up at the ceiling, letting my thoughts flow. Today is a day of many possibilities. Who knows what the outcomes of our fights will be, or when they will be for that matter. All I can do is hope that everything works out for the best. Eventually I hear the ever familiar sound of our alarm go off, and Clarence silences it immediately. The time has come. We both get up, and start getting ready. After a few minutes pass there is a knock that the door. Clarence opens the door to reveal an orderly on the other side. "Twenty-four minutes until the train leaves, don't be late," he says. And with that he's gone, off to the next room I'm sure.

Clarence and I get ready and make our way to the entrance. There is a line, just like last time, only it seems slightly larger this time. Probably because we didn't get out of our room as fast as we did last time. We stand in line for a short while and eventually scan in and board the train, and before long we are at the arena once again.

We are escorted to the waiting room, everything is exactly the same as it was. The giant projection on the wall, the buffet in the middle of the room, and the black couches and chairs against the walls. Clarence and I walk in and head directly to the food table to

164

eat some super food. Since we are repeat contenders we know that there is no chance of us fighting right away. We will likely be one of the last fights. After we grab the food we look around for a spot to sit, and I spot a familiar face entering the room with the last of the people from our group. "Hey man look, there's Joseph," I say.

"Nice! Now we can hang out 'til he has to fight."

I wave at Joseph to get his attention. He sees us and his face lights up joy as he makes his way to us. "Hey guys! So you got the knock after all, huh?

"Yeah it seems that way," Clarence says, "one step closer and all.

"How are you feeling?" I ask.

"Not too bad, I'm a little nervous, but I'm sure I'll be able to pull it together when the time comes. I just hope that I don't have to wait all day to fight like you guys probably will."

"Yeah I'm not excited to sit here and wait, but at least we know that we have time and don't have to be ready to go at a moment's notice like you," I say.

"You gonna grab some food?" Clarence asks.

"I might snack, don't wanna eat too much since I don't know when I'm gonna be up."

"Yeah that's what we did last time," I say.

"Cool thing is if you go early enough you get to chill in the victor's lounge with all the pretty lady victors," Clarence says.

"Yeah Gordon mentioned that, I don't know if I'll even talk to them though to be honest. I'll probably just watch the fights, I don't think I could really talk to girls wearing this skimpy outfit."

"I don't know why not man, you look like a freak beast," Clarence states.

"Yeah whatever, I guess I'll just have to wait and see. Maybe." Joseph's face turns a little red and we laugh.

"Let's grab a seat somewhere," I say.

"Good idea," Joseph says. We make our way to the far side of the room from the entrance and settle in the middle. We sit facing towards the food table and the projector is to our right so we can still watch the fights. The opening ceremony should be starting soon. "Any advice for me before things get going?"

"Not really man," Clarence responds, "you've just gotta go out there and give it your all. Throw it all out there and leave it on the table. See what happens, you know? I'm sure you'll kick some serious butt."

"Yeah man," I add, "just give it your all because that's all you can do. You've got this."

"I figured you would say something like that, but I just wanted to ask just in case there was some secret to it all." He laughs awkwardly and scratches the back of his head. I don't think I've ever seen Joseph this nervous before, I can tell the waiting is killing him. It probably doesn't help that he had to wait all week to get here, and now he has to wait even more to actually fight. While I would like it if he was a later fight like us so he can sit and spend more time with us, I also want it to happen soon for his sake. I don't think he could handle waiting until this evening to fight.

Our conversation is interrupted by the sound of the opening sequence for the show, the entire room grows quiet as the music starts and the show commences. I didn't even notice the orderlies come and retrieve the first combatant. Once the beginning comes to and end the same two faces that are there for every show come on. "Hello everyone, and welcome back to another exciting day in 'The Arena', I'm Charles Platt and alongside me is Blake Lewis." I think I like these two less every time I see them now. Especially because I know they are going to be commenting on my every move when I'm in combat.

"Yes Charles it looks like it is going to be another beautiful day for a little bit of blood shed as the first week of the new season comes to a close, and with its close we have a special surprise for some of our viewers."

"What's that Blake?"

"Well, we're going to be bringing back some of the victors from a few of the best matches this week to face off for the second time in their careers! Just a special way to end things with a bang!"

"That sounds just great Blake, I'm looking forward to it. But before we can get there, we have plenty of other great matches to get through first!"

"Did it feel different for you guys too?" Joseph asks.

"What do you mean?" Clarence asks.

"Seeing the show start on a day that you're actually fighting. I've seen it countless times before, but this time just feels more intense, heavier."

"That's how I felt last time we were here," I say. "Now I just get annoyed with the announcers because I think about what they might be saying while we're fighting."

"I'm sure everything will be fine," Joseph says, "it just feels more real now that I'm here. Before it was always something that would happen eventually, but it felt like it never would. Here we are though."

"You can't let anything get to you man," Clarence says. "You just need to focus up, and when the time comes be ready to go out there and win. You do whatever you have to do, I don't care. You can even pull a Gordon and do cheap shots if that's what it takes to make it through. Just do what you have to do to make it to that victors lounge and we'll meet you there after, okay?"

"You make it sound easy," Joseph responds. "I'll do my best, I'm sure it's going to be fine." He says with a smile.

A couple of hours pass, and the room empties out little by little as the competitors all go to face their foes. Finally, at around 11:30 am I hear the voice of an orderly utter the name we've been waiting for, "Joseph."

"Well this is it guys," Joseph says. "Wish me luck."

"You've got this man," I say.

"LET'S GO!" Clarence yells, "LET'S GO! YOU GOT THIS MAN! LET'S GO LET'S GO! GET PUMPED! GET PSYCHED!" he screams as his smacks Joseph on the back. "GET ANGRY! GET MEAN! GET TOUGH! THIS IS YOU, THIS IS YOUR MOMENT, THIS IS YOUR TIME, NOW GO TAKE IT!"

Joseph lights up after hearing Clarence's words, you can see the fire growing in his eyes. "Yeah! I've got this! I can do this! I'll see you guys on the other side, thanks for everything guys." He gives a half grin that matches the fire in his eyes as he starts to make his way towards the door. As he walks through and the door starts to close I see him spin around and give a full Joseph smile and wave. I only see it for a moment before the door shuts, and he's gone. Now we have to wait and see what happens. It's in his hands now.

XI

Waiting for Joseph to walk out into the arena feels like a lifetime. His match should be after the one that is currently taking place, it's a female doubles match. I know that it's only minutes away, but time seems to have a tendency to drag when I'm nervous about something. He's the last of my friends to fight, and I have no idea how he will handle himself out there. I have full faith in his abilities, but the waiting game is never fun. I hated it when Gordon had to fight, I hated it when Clarence and I had to fight, and I hate it now. The one positive thing that is coming out of this is that it makes it easier to not think about our fight that will be coming up later today. I'm staring at the screen, but I'm not really watching what's going on. I'm just spacing out lost in my own thoughts.

"Ooh! And another gory finish!" Charles says. I focus in to see the two victors standing in the middle of the arena with their hands in the air cheering with fierce victory faces standing next to a decapitated body. It won't be long now.

"You're right about that one Charles," Blake says. "It was a real nail biter for the start of the fight, could have gone either way, but it looks like Jasmine and Katheryn came out on top of this one nearly unscathed."

"Yeah I tell you what though, Katheryn is going to be feeling a few of those blows to the stomach and head tomorrow. Somebody give that girl a pain pill, yikes!"

"Well we only have a few more new contenders left on the docket for today before we get into our repeat matches folks."

"So get yourselves ready for the next contestants as they step into the spotlight for the first time. The next two contenders will be Joseph, and Kyle! Stay tuned!" Joseph is only a few moments away from getting things going.

"Now it may be their first time fighting, and these two may have been middle of the pack in the academy, but don't let that fool you. I've seen some of the best fights from guys like them when you least expect it," Charles says.

"Not to mention, we don't really know what crazy training regimen they've been following since they left the academy. Who knows where their skill level lies now. I remember back a few seasons ago when Quinton was nothing but a mediocre silver level gladiator coming into the arena, but after a few matches he started moving up the ladder until he sat atop the diamond competitors. You can never tell what you're going to get out of guys like this."

"Well I think that's enough talk for now Blake, let's bring 'em out!"

"Ladies and gentlemen your next combatants are about to enter the arena!"

They introduce Kyle first. He stands tall, about 6'3" with a thin stature. He has light brown hair that stands a few inches off his head and waves in the gentle breeze that sweeps through the arena with a small beard just long enough to cover his skin on the bottom of his cheeks, down his jawline, and around his mouth. He pays no mind to the crowd, he just walks straight towards the center of the arena without even looking at his surroundings. He has the demeanor of a more seasoned gladiator even though it's only his first match. Maybe it's part of his plan to try to intimidate Joseph.

They call Joseph's name next. As the doors open and he sets foot onto the arena for the first time he looks completely serious and stern. The most serious I think I've ever seen him in my life. To this point he has always been the one that smiles to bring everyone else up around him, but right now I can tell he means business. He's focused, and he appears ready for whatever Kyle is about to throw at him. The sunlight shines off Joseph's green eyes making them look lighter than normal, his face doesn't even resemble the Joseph I know right now. He's someone else entirely, someone tougher, someone stronger.

The two reach the middle of the arena and stare at each other for a moment before shaking hands, neither of them has any change in their face at all. Kyle towers over Joseph by six inches, which must feel intimidating. He must have prepared for larger foes, since he isn't the tallest by any means.

They turn away from one another now and place their heels back to back. It's about to begin. "Ladies and Gentlemen, without further ado, let us begin! In three…!" Charles says. This is it, this is Joseph's moment. Make or break time. Here we go. "TWO…ONE…BEGIN!"

The moment the words leave Charles' lips the two of them start running in opposite directions, neither of them try to do anything crazy at the start. Joseph reaches the edge of the arena just moments before Kyle does, not that it matters since they are on opposite sides. Joseph grabs his weapon of choice, the meteor hammer which is basically two weights connected by a long chain, this one has a head similar to a mace. Kyle retrieves two gladiator dolch swords. The two turn and face each other as they start to slowly make their way back towards one another.

Joseph takes a defensive stance as the gap grows smaller between them, keeping the chain taught between his hands, ready to react. They draw closer and closer until only a few body lengths apart. Kyle lunges forward, stabbing at Joseph with one of his swords. Joseph quickly reacts by stepping sideways and wrapping the sword in his chain and ripping it away from Kyle, disarming him. I can't help but smile as I see Joseph getting the better of his opponent. Kyle backs away immediately as Joseph releases the sword he just stole to the ground and kicks it away. Joseph starts to spin one end of the meteor hammer, he's preparing to take the offensive.

Kyle switches hands with his remaining blade, placing it in his right hand. He doesn't appear to want to be forced into a defensive stance, so instead he charges at Joseph again. This time jumping into the air and bring his sword down with both of his hands as he yells. Joseph simultaneously swings the head of his weapon to his right, around the left side of Kyle, as he dives right and the hammer collides with Kyle's ribs. I can hear the sound of Kyle's ribs crack as the weapon strikes flesh. Kyle comes crashing into the ground and the crowd goes wild. Severe pain is evident on Kyle's face as he brings himself to his feet. He holds his sword in his left hand and clutches his ribs with his right. There's no blood, but immediate discoloration where the damage was inflicted.

Joseph looks calm and serious as ever, he isn't taking any chances by getting overly aggressive. Joseph starts to spin a head of his weapon again. Kyle regains his composure and grabs the sword with both hands this time, taking a defensive stance. Joseph starts to slowly move towards Kyle. Crouching a little, but not seceding any ground, Kyle waits for Joseph to make his move. Joseph lets the spinning head fly from his left hand, coming around Kyle's right side and Kyle counters it with his sword, blocking the head. As he does this however, Joseph swings the right head up with great force and it collides with Kyle's jaw on the left side of his face. The blow lets loose another loud crack of bone as Kyle leaves his feet, falling backwards. Droplets of blood spew into the air as a mist with chunks of teeth mixed in. Kyle's body hits the ground and his sword leaves his hand. He coughs and more blood and teeth leave his mouth.

Joseph still has no emotion on his face, just the fierce look in his glowing green eyes. He starts to spin the right side of his weapon and takes a step forward as his arm extends overhead and he brings the hammer crashing down into Kyle's knee, bending it backwards. Kyle lets out a blood curdling scream that only feeds the crowd more. Within a moment, before Kyle can even begin to think to react, Joseph spins the other head of his weapon and brings it overhead only to have it crush Kyle's other knee. Kyle is done for. He can't walk, he can't barely breathe between spitting out chunks of blood and teeth. It appears to be over.

Kyle attempts to crawl away, making his way towards his sword that fell a few feet away from him. He isn't giving up. Joseph doesn't let him get far though. Just as Kyle starts to move Joseph stomps his right foot into Kyle's back, pinning him to the ground. Joseph then proceeds to reach down and wrap the middle of the chain around Kyle's throat before pulling back on both sides of the chain with all of his might as he presses against Kyle's back with his foot. Joseph starts to yell as he does this. All of the veins start to bulge from Kyle's neck and face, and his eyeballs become bloodshot and look as though they might leave his skull. Kyle frantically starts blindly reaching towards the sword he was trying to make it to with his right hand. His fingertips brush the base of the hilt but he can't quite grasp it. He paws at it like a wild animal as his face grows

173

redder than I thought possible for a man. Joseph screams louder as he looks up at the sky as though he's yelling to the clouds and pulls even more, sliding his foot sideways and pressing it as hard as he can against his opponent's back. Kyle's fingertips finally find traction in the hilt and he manages to slide it towards him. In his final moments, after what seems like an eternity he grasps the handle in his right hand and flips the blade before blindly stabbing backwards directly between the two lengths of chain that Joseph is pulling from. The blade goes directly through Joseph's calf, severing all ties between bone and muscle cutting it completely. The top part of Josephs calf slingshots up into his knee and he starts to fall sideways, a look of disbelief and pain on his face. Kyle takes his first breath after what he thought would be his last breath, and starts to cough violently for a moment as Joseph falls to the ground.

Joseph hits the ground and his face lights up with pain, but he knows the fight is still going. He looks towards Kyle, who is now at the base of his feet. Joseph uses his arms to roll himself over, seemingly ignoring his now mangled leg. Kyle is still coughing, trying to recover. Joseph throws himself toward Kyle and grabs one head of his meteor hammer and starts to pull it to regain control of his weapon. Kyle feels the chain sliding and realizes what is happening. He does his best to regain what little composure he can and grabs his sword. Joseph grabs a length of chain and attempts to swing the hammer he has control of as he lays but a foot away from Kyle, their bodies in the shape of a V. Before Joseph can manage to get any momentum behind the hammer Kyle grasps his sword in his left hand, and uses all of his energy to roll onto his back as he brings the tip of the sword into Joseph's flesh just behind his collar bone, in front of his scapula, and he buries the blade in Joseph's chest cavity. Joseph's face lights up like someone who was just surprised or frightened. Within moments the light fades from his eyes, where there once was a glow there is now only darkness. His body goes limp, it's over.

My heart stops. I can't breathe. I can't move. I can't do anything. This isn't supposed to happen, this isn't how things are supposed to play out. Joseph had it, he had won, how did this happen? Joseph can't be gone. We made a promise to each other, we are all supposed to make it out, all of us. How am I supposed to go out there and fight knowing that I won't see him again? I'll never again see that smile that always brightened my day and made me feel better. It feels as though there's a giant hole that has just been ripped out of my chest. I want to speak, but my throat feels constricted. My vision is blurry, and my cheeks feel wet.

"I know it hurts," Clarence says softly, "but this isn't the time for us to deal with this. We can't afford to lose focus."

"I..." I try to speak but choke on my own words.

"You have thirty seconds, that's it. After that we move on. You can think about Joseph later. Real men don't cry." Thirty seconds? That's all? How am I supposed to process everything that's happened and be okay in just thirty seconds? How am I supposed to carry on right now? Joseph has always been there. Always. How does one simply forget all of that in thirty seconds? "I know it hurts, but you need to just push it down. Take that pain in your chest, ball it up, compress it, and shove it way down deep where you can't feel it anymore. Turn it off." I'm so lost right now, and I don't know how Clarence is keeping his composure so well, but I know he's right.

I wipe the tears from my cheeks and look at Clarence, his face is stern and cold. He may be better at hiding it, but I can tell he's feeling everything that I am right now. So I take that hole that has been ripped open in my chest, and I compress it as much as possible. I shove it down inside me where I can't feel it as much, and I leave it there. I can process everything later. Normally I can just shrug things off and avoid my problems, but this is so much harder than anything I've felt before. I can't even remember the last time I cried.

I know this isn't just about me right now, if I lose focus in our fight I won't only be getting me killed, but Clarence too. The pain is still there, but I have to ignore it and just pretend that it isn't for the time being. If I ignore it enough, maybe it will hurt less eventually. "Okay," I say quietly. "You're right, there's time for this later."

"Clarence and Royce," a voice calls from across the room. I look over to see an orderly standing in the doorway. Is it really our time? Now of all times? There really is no choice but to bottle everything up and pretend it didn't happen, we are only a few minutes away from our fight.

"Let's go man," Clarence says, still speaking softly. "We have business to take care of." I nod at him and stand up. We both walk towards the orderly. He escorts us through the door and leads us to the final waiting room. The cement halls seem darker and duller than they did before on the walk. The halls seem deafeningly quiet, I can't even hear the sound of our footsteps. All I can hear is a ringing in my ears as we walk. I stare blankly ahead, I feel nothing but a slight ache in the bottom of my chest. There is no fear, there is no anger, there is no sadness or happiness, I'm just empty. I don't even look at Clarence or the orderly the entire time, I just blankly stare ahead zoned out and unfocused on anything, just going through the motions. I don't even will my legs to move, they seem to just be walking on their own.

We finally arrive at the final waiting room and go inside. The orderly says something to us, but I don't listen. I can't hear him right now. It's taking everything I have to not think about what just happened. I notice the door close out of my peripherals, I sit on a bench and stare blankly at the floor.

I hear mumbling but pay no attention to it at first, it grows louder and louder, but still I don't focus. "HEY!" Clarence screams at me, snapping me out of my haze. I look up at him. "I know you're messed up right now okay? But now isn't the time. I get it, Joseph is gone and it sucks, it sucks a lot. You know what though? Crying about it won't change anything. Now I'm not gonna sit here and try to get you amped up about the fight. I'm not gonna tell you what you have to do out there, because you should already know. I'm not even gonna ask you to try and put on a fake smile for the crowd. What I am going to do though, is remind you that it isn't just you out there, it's both of us. I need you. So what you're going to do is stop crying and moping, and get pissed. Get angry. Get MAD! Our best friend just got murdered in front of us, in front of the world! Everyone saw it, and they enjoyed it. Those sick people in that crowd enjoyed watching him die. That pisses me off, and it should piss you off too. You can mourn his death later, but right now I need you angry. I need you so mad that you are going to go out there and literally kill the guy in front of you. Get mad, get pissed, get heated, and take it out on whoever sets foot on that arena opposite us. Take all of your frustrations out on them. Got it!?" I can hear the anger boiling inside of Clarence coming through in his voice, hearing his words ignites something inside of me too.

He's right, I shouldn't be sad that Joseph is gone, I should be mad. I am mad. I'm angry. I'm pissed that they took him away from me. I'm upset that I won't be able to see his smile again. I'm furious that they took one of my best friends' life from him, and now they want to try and take mine. I won't sit here and mope anymore, I'm going to go out there and show them just how angry I am. I'm going to tear whoever is in front of me to shreds. I'm going to make them wish they had faced literally any other opponent, because I'm going to be their last. I'm going to take a life because a life was taken from me. And I'm going to enjoy it. It may not bring Joseph back, but I have to do something with all this pain I'm feeling. So I'm going to take it out on them. "Let's do this," I say with a slight growl to my voice. I can feel my heartbeat begin to rise, along with my temperature. I want to hit something, I want to break something, I want to let out everything pent up inside me, and I'm about to be given the opportunity to do so.

The doors start to slowly open and I can hear the roar of the crowd. I rise to my feet and face them. "For Joseph," Clarence says, extending his fist towards me.

"For Joseph," I say back as I meet his fist with mine.

177

We set foot into the arena and make our way to the center. Opposite us I can see our opponents doing the same. I recognize one of them, it's Scott from my spear class. This only makes me angrier, the guy I hated most in class is now my opponent. This is too perfect. I'm finally going to show him I'm the better of us. "That's Scott," I say to Clarence as we make our way towards the middle. "He's from my spear class, he's good so be ready."

"That's Tannis," Clarence says. "He was in my sword class, I whooped on him regularly, but he was still better than most of the others. Looks like they planned this as some sort of sick twist. Sword and spear versus sword and spear. Be ready."

"I don't care who they are or what they think they're going to do, they're not the ones who are going to be walking away from this."

We meet them in the middle and lock eyes for a moment, Scott opposite me and Tannis opposite Clarence. Tannis is roughly 5'9" with a clean shaven head, no hair on his entire body aside from his eyebrows and eyelashes. He has dark brown eyes and a pointed jawline and chin. Scott has grown his crew cut out a little and spiked it, everything else remains the same though. His eyes are still brown, he's still 6'2", and I'm guessing he still has an aggravating attitude. He smirks at me, I can tell he thinks he's better than me, but not today. We shake hands, and turn away from one another, placing our heels back to back. I look ahead to see what my options are. There is a glaive right next to two dolch swords, perfect for Clarence and I. It may not be a spear, but they are similar enough and I've used a glaive in the past.

"IN THREE..." Blake says over the intercom. I look to Clarence and nod; he does the same. "TWO..." I focus back in on my destination. "ONE..." I take a deep breath and exhale. This is for Joseph. "BEGIN!"

Clarence and I both do our standard start and leap into our handspring. Looking back, I see Tannis and Scott tumbling forward, a similar strategy to ours. We return to our feet and start sprinting towards our weapons. Once we reach the wall I grab the glaive and Clarence acquires his swords, we look back and see that Scott has a spear and Tannis has two scimitars. Of course they would get our preferred weapons. The two of them start to slowly make their way towards us, as we do the same. As they close the gap they separate, walking diagonally away from each other and moving towards opposite sides of the arena. "I'll take Tannis," Clarence says as he starts to head off to the right to meet him.

"Sounds good," I say as I head to the left to meet Scott. As soon as we do this they stop moving apart and run back together and switch sides. They must want the mismatch. "You good? Clarence yells.

"I got him," I holler back. I don't care who I'm facing I just want to hurt someone.

Tannis slows to a walk once he's established he wants to fight me and we make our way towards one another. I stand ready with my glaive in both hands, the butt end in my left hand and the head in my right. Tannis draws closer and closer until he finally decides to get aggressive, he accelerates, taking a wide stance and hopping back and forth running towards me. I run at him as well. Once he is only a few body lengths away from me he leaps into the air, raising both of his swords over his head planning to bring them down on me. I slide down on my back and bring the glaive up over me blocking his strike and raise my feet to kick him in the thigh, using his momentum to send him flying in the opposite direction of me.

I jump back to my feet and turn to see him doing the same. He brushes some dirt off of his shoulder and rolls his head around, popping his neck. He comes again. This time he runs at me and only brings one blade up to strike, so I prepare to block again, but he brings the blade in his right hand around my left side in an attempt to catch me off guard. I slide the top of my weapon up to meet his first strike and plant the base to deflect the second before making it perpendicular to the ground in order to use it to lift myself off the ground and swing my body around to the right. Both of his blades meet my glaive as I come around behind him and knee him in the center of his back. He drops his sword from his left hand as he stumbles and falls to the ground. I use this opportunity to glance across the arena to see Clarence fighting Scott, who blocks one of Clarence's attacks and brings the base of his spear around to strike Clarence in his left knee, staggering him. Clarence may need me, I have to finish this.

I look back to Tannis, who grabs the sword he dropped and rises back to his feet. He shakes it off. Behind him I can still see Clarence and Scott fighting, Clarence is slightly favoring his left knee. I have to take the offensive. I charge at Tannis and slide the glaive out until my left hand is at the very base before bringing it around his left side in an attempt to strike him. He turns and blocks it with both of his swords just below the blade. As he does this I plant my feet and slide forward, to the right of him and pull the glaive back and swinging the head down and butt up. His swords are caught by the blade and it disarms him. I then raise the head and slide it immediately forward towards his midsection. He turns away from it to his left, sliding his right side forward and the blade grazes him across his stomach, drawing blood. The wound isn't deep but it's a start.

Tannis grabs the glaive behind the axe and attempts to pull on it to disarm me, but I don't let go. I pull back, but he won't yield either. He starts to back peddle, causing me to shift directions, but still I don't let go. He looks over my shoulder towards the others and screams. I want to look to see what he's screaming at but I can't afford to look away with my weapon locked in his hands. I pull again, but it's no use. He continues to try and shift me, so I plant my feet and push to my left and pull with my right with all of my might. He loses his balance and falls forward, letting go of the glaive. I raise it over my head, this is my opportunity to finish it. He glances up and smirks for some reason. I start to bring the head of the glaive down and am stopped as a searing pain meets my right shoulder blade and finds its way through my chest, knocking me off balance and causing me to drop my weapon. I look down in disbelief to see the tip of a spear sticking out of my chest just to the left of my shoulder. I try to breathe, but it hurts and I can't seem to find any air. I don't understand what has happened as I fall to my knees in disbelief and shock. I look back at Tannis as he stands up and runs over to his swords. I assume he's going to come and end me, but instead he starts to run across the arena to the left of where we were. Where's Clarence? Where's Scott? What happened? I don't understand. I see my own blood dripping off of the spear that is now a part of my body and I can't hardly move. I look over to see Clarence being met by Tannis as he chases Scott, who has no weapon. Tannis tosses one of his swords to Scott and they start to corner Clarence. I have to do something.

I try to reach behind my left shoulder with my right hand, but I can't, and in doing so I can feel my insides tearing from the motion. I can't fight with a spear in my shoulder and I can't pull it out from the back. I grab the spear with my left hand from the front instead, just behind the tip and pull with all my might. It starts to move and blood starts to pour out me, I scream in agony, but it doesn't stop me. I slide my hand down the blood soaked spear and grab hold in order to pull again. The spear slowly slides through my body, one forearm length at a time. I've never felt such immense pain in my life, but Clarence needs me, so I keep going. Eventually I manage to free the spear from my body causing it to fall to the ground, and the pain intensifies as blood begins to run freely from my body. I grab the blood drenched spear and stagger to my feet. I stand unsteady, swaying side to side, I doubt if I can even walk. I look to see flashes of Clarence defending himself against Scott and Tannis. Using every ounce of strength I have left in my body I raise the spear over my left shoulder and attempt to run forward towards them. Screaming at the top of my lungs I throw my entire body into releasing the spear and fall to the ground as it becomes airborne. My limp body hits the dirt and I see a puddle starting to accrue on my right side. I look up, laying face down on the ground, growing colder and colder. I can no longer feel the pain, I can't feel anything. My vision is cutting in and out, it's like a strobe effect as I see my spear flying towards my opponents. I can no longer keep my eyes open, they force themselves shut and I hear the crowd erupt into a great roar moments later. I start to relax, I don't know why I'm relaxed, but I am. I hear what sounds like the muffled voices of the announcers, they are excited about something. I want to listen to what it is, but I can't focus. I'm drifting off, I'm no longer capable of doing anything, even listening. I feel the most tired I've ever been in my life, my body just wants to sleep. Every part of me is saying go to sleep, let go. I want to let go. I might let go. I think I'll just let go.

XII

"No!" I scream at the top of my lungs as I violently sit up in a bed of some sort. My heart is racing; I have no idea what's happening. I'm confused, and light headed, and my heart might fight its way out of my chest at any second. Was I sleeping? How did I get here? I take a moment to look around and see that I'm in a small room with a lot of equipment hooked up to my arms and chest. I appear to be wearing some sort of thin cloth gown.

"Good evening Royce," A slightly raspy voice says from across the room. I look to my right and see a man standing in the doorway wearing all white with rectangular glasses, a pale complexion, and short light gray hair. "My name is Doctor Schmidt, and I have to say you are a very lucky young man." Lucky? What's he talking about?

"Okay?" I say confused.

"Tell me, what is the last thing you remember?"

"Well..." I have to pause and think for a moment. What is the last thing I remember? "I was bleeding. The spear!" I exclaim as I reach for my right shoulder where the hole was. The hole is gone, it's as if it was never there. "Clarence!" I yell, I just remembered he was still fighting when I went down. "Is he okay!?"

"Your friend is fine, better than fine actually. The two of you are quite popular after winning that fight the way you did."

"Wait, we won?"

"Oh yes, it was quite miraculous actually. Just when everyone had counted you out you managed to remove that spear from your shoulder in quite possibly the most painful manner possible. A clear-headed individual might have just thrust their chest onto the ground to push the spear back and make it easier to remove from its weight alone. You however, decided to pull the entire thing through your body before somehow finding the strength to grab it and hurl it at not only your enemies, but your cornered teammate. This is the truly interesting part, you nearly missed. In fact, I thought you would miss completely, but you managed to graze the inner thigh near the groin of Scott and sever his femoral artery. He bled out right before everyone's eyes. Your friend Clarence then had his way with Tannis one on one and emerged victorious. In fact, I don't know what's more interesting about this story. The fact that the two of you managed to win, or the fact that you're still alive. You managed to tear most of the muscles in your shoulder area, fracture your scapula, and puncture a lung. But you somehow didn't tear a single artery. That coupled with what I can only call a strong desire to live, or being too stubborn to die, is what kept you alive. The hidden beauty in all of this too is that you are one of the few gladiators to ever be credited with a kill while unconscious. I personally have never seen anything like it. Everyone's talking about you boys now."

"Where is Clarence now?"

"Oh he's back at the training center, you'll see him soon enough. We just had to keep you here until you woke up. Injuries like that take a toll on your body, no matter how advanced our medicine is these days. It's funny, he actually refused to leave your side at first. Stayed with you all the way up until we had you in the healing chamber. He kept screaming at you, telling you not to leave him or something. As if he thought yelling at you would convince you not to die. And who knows, maybe that's what actually did it, I mean you are still here after all."

"How long have I been here?"

"About three days, the body needs to rest after going through a trauma like that."

"But I'm good now, right? I can go?"

"Yes sir, I just needed to keep you here until you woke up, all that's left for you to do now is get checked out by and orderly and they'll take you back home to the training center. If you have any questions, ask now because I have a lot of other patients to check in on and we probably won't be seeing each other for quite some time, unless you decide to do this on a regular basis that is."

"No sir, I think I just want to get back to see my friends." Saying 'friends' reminds me of Joseph. He's gone…and it hurts. I need to find some way to make sure that I don't lose any more friends, I just don't know how yet.

"Well good luck to ya then, an orderly will be here shortly." Doctor Schmidt waves as he turns and leaves the room.

An orderly enters as the doctor leaves. "Put these on," he says as he throws a set of casuals at me. I start pulling all of the things stuck to my body off and remove my gown. I raise to my feet and wobble a bit at first. I guess this is what it feels like to not walk for several days. Once I regain my composure I put the clothes on and walk towards the orderly. "Right this way," he says as he starts to walk out the door. He leads me into a beige hallway that has rails

184

on both sides and random pieces of equipment here and there. There are several doctors walking around, as well as other people wearing pink or blue uniforms. The orderly leads me to the basement. He opens the door and I see the train waiting for me. I'm starting to wonder if there is anywhere this train doesn't go.

I scan into the train and take my seat. "The train will be departing soon, please be patient." The standard intercom voice says. I can only see two other people on the entire train, and one of them is an orderly. I can't make out the other person because they are sitting many rows in front of me, but it looks like a girl. The train ride is only a couple of minutes. When it comes to a stop the person in front of me exits the train without ever looking back, I may never know who it is or what they look like. I exit the train and am back to what has become normalcy for me. A familiar place that I never thought I'd be happy to see. The ever-bland training center, complete with ever familiar white walls lined with the occasional orderly. I look up and see a clock, it's 7:55 pm. I'm not hungry for some reason, even though I haven't eaten in three days, so I decide to just head back to my room.

I open the door and see a familiar face light up, Clarence. "MY MAN!" Clarence yells. "I knew you would pull through! Nothing can bring my boy down, nothing!" He says as he hugs me and picks me up off the ground.

"Good to see you too," I say.

"How you feelin!? You good? You gave me quite the scare, I was literally yelling at you telling you not to die for a bit there."

"I'm surprisingly good, good as new."

"That's great to here man. Seeing you on the ground like that was pretty terrifying if I'm being honest. I will say though, you really came through for me when I needed you. The way you threw that spear? Amazing. I figure you weren't aiming for his leg, but hey I'll take what I can get you know?"

"Yeah I basically just threw it as hard as I could at the time and hoped for the best."

"Well it worked, and saved the match. I honestly saw you go down and it freaked me out inside. I didn't have time to process though because of the situation. I was relieved to see the spear hit him, and I thought you were somehow okay, so I finished the fight. Then I looked over at you on the ground and lost it. Don't ever do that to me again, okay?"

"Yeah I'm not planning on it. That wasn't a fun experience, to say the least. But hey, at least I'm getting all the near-death experiences out of the way early so we can just coast through the rest of our matches."

"That's one way to put it," Clarence says with a laugh. "We've got a lot of work to do still. Two down eighteen to go am I right?"

"Sounds about right."

"You need anything man? Wanna do something? We don't have to go straight to bed or anything if you wanna do something."

"I'm actually pretty tired. I don't know why, I just slept for three days, but I just am. We can start fresh in the morning."

"Yeah it's probably for the best, you need as much recovery time as you can get before we have to get back at it. I'm glad you're feelin' better man."

"Thanks, me too." I take my casuals off and climb into bed. I don't even brush my teeth or shower or any of my normal routine. I just feel exhausted for some reason. We both get in bed and turn off the lights.

"Night man."

"Goodnight Clarence."

"Two and O!"

"18 to go," I say. Just 18 more matches and we are done, 36 lives stand between us and freedom. Thinking about the fact that we have to remove 36 more people from this world in order for the two of us to have a chance at freedom makes my chest tense up, and my stomach feel sick. It never bothered me before, but now I feel it starting to weigh on me. That's 36 friends we have to kill, 36 people who might be someone's Joseph, or Gordon, or Clarence. There's a hole in my heart where Joseph belongs, a pit that hurts whenever I think about him. Are we putting others through this pain every time we win a match? I can't think about this, I need to remain focused. It's just harder when I'm alone and left with nothing but my thoughts. We need to get out of here as soon as possible so I can put this all behind me, and there's only one way to do that. "Hey Clarence."

"Yeah man?"

"Do me a favor real quick?"

"Anything you need man, you know I got you."

"Hit the button."

"You sure man? You just got back, what if you're not ready? Maybe we should take some time to make sure you're good."

"I'm sure. All that waiting around is going to do is make things harder and take longer. We need to get this done. We're only ten percent of the way there and we've already lost someone, I need to keep moving forward if I'm going to be able to make it through this. Going slow is only going to give me time to dwell on distractions and what ifs. I'll be ready by the time they call us up, we'll just have to train our hearts out."

"As long as you're sure man, I get what you mean and you know I'm down to get this done."

"I just need to keep moving forward. I feel like a shark, as long as I keep moving nothing can stop me, but if I ever stop..."

187

"Well then I guess we never stop. I like that, not only are we top dogs around here but we're sharks too huh? I can work with that. Let's get it done!" Clarence hops out of bed and walks over to the button and slams his hand down on it. "One step closer!"

"One step closer."

"Anything else you need man?" He asks.

"I'm good."

"Well you know I'm always here if you need me man, us against the world."

"I know, same goes to you."

"Man you know nothing bothers me," he says with a laugh as he climbs back into bed, "but I'll keep that in mind.

"Sounds good." Clarence and I know that we can talk to each other about anything, but there's some things that neither of us ever talk about. The really heavy stuff you just have to keep to yourself sometimes. I'm sure he feels the same way I do, and maybe talking would help, but if I talk about it I have to think about it, and that's just something that I'm not ready to do. I just have to keep going, keep progressing, keep working towards that end goal. I really do feel like a shark, as long as I keep moving nothing can stop me, it's only if I stop that I'll die. "Two down."

"Eighteen to go!" Clarence says. "Ain't nothing can stand in our way!"

"Undefeated all the way." I just have to keep telling myself that. Just eighteen more, and then seventeen, and so on. Eyes on the prize, it may be a long road but as long as we stay focused there's nothing that can stop us.

Made in the USA
Coppell, TX
27 March 2021

52434665R00111